ABOUT THIS BOOK

Every town has stories of its past, and Havenwood Falls is no different. And when the town's residents include a variety of supernatural creatures, those historical tales often become Legends. This is but one . . .

Witch hunter Marie Blackstone has always planned to follow in her mother's ways, learning to control her power and live at peace with their coven neighbors. During her first foray into playing ambassador to the witches, she meets Judson Carter. He is everything she wants in a man—and everything her brother hates.

Dante Blackstone has craved power from a young age. After the death of his and Marie's mother, his hatred for the witches grows into madness. For Dante, a witch's mere presence triggers an undeniable urge to end the creature's existence.

Seeking freedom from her brother's vendetta and to find a new way to live, Marie joins Judson and other supernatural beings as they set out in search of a new home and a new way of life. The traveling band makes its way across rough, uncharted terrain, with no idea where they're heading or how long it will take to find the perfect place.

Trouble is inevitable along the way, but for Marie, the worst comes in the form of Dante and his following of rogue witch hunters. They're intent on finding his "lost" family to bring her back into the hunter's way of life—even if that means eradicating any witch who gets in their way.

DAWN OF THE WITCH HUNTERS

A LEGENDS OF HAVENWOOD FALLS NOVELLA

MORGAN WYLIE

ALSO BY MORGAN WYLIE

YA FANTASY

Silent Orchids (Book 1)

Veiled Shadows (Book 2)

Daegan (Novella 2.5)

Fractured Darkness (Book 3)

Fading Light (Book 4)

The Sol-Lumieth (Forthcoming)

The Rise of the Paladin (An Alandria Short Story Prequel-Free with
Newsletter subscription)

YA PARANORMAL/SUPERNATURAL:: HAILEY: THE NECROMANCER (A SHADOW REALM NOVELLA 1)

JAX: The Doppelgänger (A Shadow Realm Novella 2)

WILLOW (A Shadow Realm Novella 3) (Forthcoming)

SOLANGE: (A Shadow Realm Novella 4) (Forthcoming)

NA/ADULT PARANORMAL ROMANCE:: RYLEN (THE TANGLED WEB BOOK 1)

MATHER (The Tangled Web Book 2)

JET (A Tangled Web Novella)

ENOCK (Forthcoming)

LUCIUS (Forthcoming)

ADDITIONAL COLLECTIONS:

Reawakened (A Havenwood Falls High Novella)

To YOU the readers, whether this is your first introduction to Havenwood Falls or the Blackstone family of witch hunters, or if you are already an honorary member of the town like we all wish to be, I thank you for being here!

I hope you enjoy the origins of the Blackstone family and their epic adventure across the country, searching for the place we all long to be whether in the past or present . . . Havenwood Falls.

CHAPTER 1

THE EARLY YEARS

CENTRAL VIRGINIA ~ 1840

*B*arefoot, she walked the path padded with moss from her quaint cottage home to the outskirts of a neighboring village. Cessily Blackstone had a meeting with the leader of an unsuspecting coven of witches. She needed this meeting to offer her the answers she sought. Her time was running short, and she knew it. She could feel it in her bones. Since Sarah Stronghold—the leader about to meet her—had gifted her with the ability to sense not only witches near her but also black magic in her vicinity, Cessily could discern even more within herself. Something dark bubbled in her veins. The town doctor wasn't able to help her. She hadn't told her family yet—her five young children and her beloved husband, Hank—she couldn't imagine leaving them behind. Only time and a visit with the witches—her last resort—would tell.

The grass under her toes sent soothing shivers of joy up her legs, igniting a spring in her step. Though her outlook was grim, she couldn't help but feel the life and strength of the forest around her, longing for her to commune with it. Her long blond hair flowed behind her as she headed toward the meeting place. As she drew closer, the familiar tingling in her arms gained strength. Over time, she had learned to be at peace with the unusual sensations she knew were not human characteristics. Cessily had learned to control the deep desires to seek out and kill a witch—apparently an undesired side effect of the "gift" she had been given to protect her family.

She watched her children closely as they matured. Each had developed varying degrees of the same gift, passed down through her, but thankfully diluted by the joining of her human husband. Except for her second eldest, Rodney, who seemed to be fully human. Part of the gift she'd been given allowed her to sense others similar to her as well. Cessily did her best to keep the children away from the witches until they were ready, but the three eldest—LeAnna, Rodney, and Isaiah—knew of their heritage while the two youngest, Dante and Marie, were still in the dark.

"Cessily, welcome. It has been quite some time since we last spoke," a female voice came from the other side of a tree as Cessily passed by. With a smile on her face, a woman, possibly in her sixties, wearing a long brown but lightweight cloak with a hood over her head, stepped into the pathway. Tall and willowy, she held her chin high and her head proud.

Cessily stopped and inclined her head respectfully. "It has indeed. Thank you for meeting with me, Sarah."

"How can I be of service to you?"

"Is there a way to reverse the gift you bestowed on me?" Cessily sighed. "I mean no disrespect, but I am not sure it is having the intended effect as it is passed down to my children. They are reacting differently, each one."

Sarah frowned, but kept her eyes trained on Cessily, clearly debating something. "No, I'm afraid it is permanent, Cessily."

"Is there anything that can be done to help ease the strongest of the desires for my children? Please don't misunderstand. I am grateful for how you helped me long ago. But I fear for my children. If they are not able to control the gift as I have learned to do, they might let it get the best of them."

"I told you when I awakened this power within you that it would not be an easy road. It is more a responsibility than a gift. You must instruct your children the way I instructed you." Sarah's gaze searched Cessily's face. "What is it you're not telling me, Cessily?"

Cessily scratched at the back of her neck and turned her head slightly, as if listening to something.

"I don't have much time. I think I am dying, Sarah," she said, her voice lowered. "And I've seen darkness in a couple of my children as the gift awakens within them. I'm scared for them."

"Give me your hand," Sarah demanded, holding out her own palm face up. Cessily placed her hand palm up within Sarah's. Sarah studied it, drew her index finger along Cessily's life line, and frowned. A lone tear escaped one of her eyes. "It is true. I am sorry, Cessily."

"Is there anything you can do? Any magic that could delay my end? Anything?" Cessily pleaded, desperation escaping her tone. "I'm not ready to die," she whispered.

Sarah reached out her other hand and placed it tenderly against Cessily's cheek. "I am truly sorry. There is nothing I can do. It is the way of nature, and I cannot interfere, even if I could do something."

"I understand."

"There is more you need to understand . . . more I have not told you about your past, Cessily." Sarah's words were slow, hesitant, with a weight Cessily didn't comprehend.

"What is it?" Cessily frowned and tilted her head, watching Sarah struggle with something internally.

"This gift . . . this power you believe I gave you . . ."

"Yes?" Cessily was concerned. A strange sensation crept up her spine, and chills erupted across her skin.

"I was not the giver. I led you to believe I gave it to you."

"If you did not, who did? What aren't you telling me now, Sarah?"

"No one did. Unless you count your ancestors, that is." Sarah sighed and stepped back from Cessily to gain some needed space. "Cessily, the power you feel, struggle with, gain insight from—your ancestors are the source of it. You are a hunter . . . a witch hunter, to be precise."

"What? You did something, though. I could feel the power flow through me when you blessed me all those years ago," Cessily said, doubt flooding her words.

"Your power was dormant. All I did was awaken the power within you."

"No. I don't believe you. I felt something come alive from your power. Why would I never know about such a huge anomaly in my family? Why would no one ever tell me? My parents never said anything!" Cessily paced, her hands worrying themselves into a frenzy.

"Your grandparents asked my mother, the coven leader at the time, to inactivate their powers when they first arrived here from Europe and to never speak of it again. It took very strong magic. It is all written in this journal I brought for you. My mother had it hidden, but I recently found it amongst her things." From beneath her cloak, Sarah brought out a worn leather book, tied and bound with a long strip of red suede. She held it out for Cessily to take.

Cessily froze, all but her eyes as they took in the little book.

"Could it really belong to my family? Could it hold all the secrets you speak of?" she whispered, but doubt laced her tone. Moving slowly closer, she squinted and peered at the ancient tome. Cessily gasped. Her eyes widened in surprise. "I recognize this symbol on the spine."

Sarah turned it to see the spine, then handed it to Cessily, who examined it more thoroughly. "This cluster of stars on the spine is also on my shoulder and on each of the children except Rodney."

"Then it truly belongs to you," Sarah acknowledged.

"You knew all along then? Back when you offered me a gift of protection?" Cessily frowned, attempting to absorb all the information just thrown at her.

Sarah slowly nodded. "I did. What my nephew . . . what that man did to you, using black magic, was unforgivable. The anger you could have allowed into your soul would have awoken your hunter in an unpleasant way. You would have been overrun with the hunger and desire to hunt and kill all witches. I chose to awaken you in a way to be distinguished as a gift, instead of a reaction to hatred. It allowed you to control and learn your hunting powers more easily. That was my restitution to you, not the actual power."

Cessily gave a small smile. "I still am grateful for the sacrifice and offering you made to me and my family. I might not be here otherwise." She sighed and noted the bright morning sun streaking down through the tree branches, a glimmer of hope in a confusing time. "Do you know much else about my ancestors?"

"It is all in the book. Read it. I will be here if you still want to talk when you are finished."

Cessily nodded. She slanted her head slightly down and to the right, listening, pausing. Her eyebrows pinched, and she bit her lip in concern. "Thank you. I should go. I sense little ones of mine who should not be here."

"Blessed be, Cessily Blackstone."

"Blessed be, Sarah Stronghold." Cessily tucked the book protectively to her chest and headed back toward home.

As she passed the patch of full green shrubbery, she didn't stop and she didn't acknowledge the children except to say, "Best hurry along so your daddy doesn't catch you away from your chores for too long."

Cessily kept walking, enjoying everything around her. The flowers woke to greet the day, the sun warmed the path beneath her toes, and the birds and chipmunks greeted each other with friendly chatter. The bush behind her jostled, and the sounds of running feet thudded away from her. She knew her youngest children, Dante and Marie, would have plenty of questions for her when they next saw her. In fact, Cessily had questions of her own. Skirting by the small trickling creek near their home, she found a nice flat boulder in the sun to sit. So she did, and she opened her family's recorded history—the only one she was aware of—and read.

~

WITHIN THE WEEK, Cessily weakened in both body and mind. Her illness consumed her from the inside out. She had little time left. Her husband Henry Jackson Blackstone—known to his friends as Hank—was one of the most understanding and patient humans she had ever known. He came along her side and lovingly wrapped an arm around her waist, assisting her with his strength. His bright green eyes gazed down upon her face with love and sadness. Her face showed she was slipping away.

"Cess, you need to tell everything to the little ones—share the new information you have learned with them all. Soon," her husband encouraged. He walked with her through the fields behind their cottage with rows and rows of vegetables. Barefoot once more, and as she usually was, Cessily nodded her head in quiet response.

Her family had been excellent farmers before she had grown and married, but Hank had added his expertise of growing grapes to turn into wine. When Cessily married Hank, he understood all she was, including her "extra" abilities. When Sarah, the coven leader, had blessed her with her gifts—or awakened her hunting side, as she now understood—she had made Cessily promise to always keep the Blackstone name prominent in her family. Until now, Cessily hadn't understood those instructions were straight out of her ancestors' book; though she still wasn't sure why, she had kept up the tradition. Hank was so head over heels in love with his new bride, he didn't care what his name was.

"I will tell them tonight. I fear I will not be here much longer, Hank. I'm afraid to leave you and the children behind." Resting her head in the crook of his shoulder, she allowed the tears she had held at bay most of the week to flow.

Everything was happening too fast. She had just found out all about her heritage, and it gave such new meaning to who she was. Was it better to allow her children to believe their abilities were the result of a gift or something that has always been and always would be a part of their lives? It now made sense why her "gift" also functioned at times as a curse, an obstacle she needed to overcome or learn to control. The power, the abilities, the drive—they were all simply a part of her, her nature. If she was honest with herself, she wasn't sure if she would take that nature away from her children, even if she could. Would life be that much easier and better for them if they didn't have to handle being witch hunters? Probably, but it was their family's responsibility, their destiny. Would she change it? No. Would she make it easier if she could? Yes. It was the most challenging part of her nature. But she needed to prepare her children for what was to come.

CHAPTER 2

"*M*ama, you don't look so well," a young Marie Blackstone, at the ripe age of ten, commented as she stormed into her mother's room of their comfortable home, a moderate-sized log cabin in Virginia passed down from Cessily's parents. She had no other siblings to share it with —though she did have cousins nearby—so she and her family were blessed to live in it after her parents passed from this life.

"I have some things I need to share with you all. Go and get your brothers and sister, Marie. Hurry along, now." Cessily coughed as she pulled herself to a partial sitting position in order to see her children's faces. Marie paused at the door, watching her mother, concern written all over her. Little Marie's face paled next to her thin blond hair running down her back and tied with a ribbon. Marie ran.

Mere moments later, Marie came running back in after rounding up her siblings.

"Mama, here they come!" she shouted and bounced over to sit on the side of the bed where her daddy usually slept.

"Good girl, Marie."

"Should I get Daddy, too?" the little girl added.

"Not just yet. This is business I have special with just you kids." Cessily stroked her hand weakly down Marie's face, and her daughter nuzzled in closer at the contact.

"Come in, Dante." Cessily beckoned him from the doorway, where he stood stiffly. His face paled, and his eyes were glued to his mother as they filled with naked fear. She patted the bed once more, but he only came to the foot of the bed and perched on the edge of it.

"LeAnna, Rodney, and Isaiah, fill in here as best you can and find somewhere to be comfortable for a few minutes. I have something to share with you all."

"What is it, Mama? Are you going to tell Dante and Marie about our gift?" LeAnna, the eldest child, asked with the air of one who felt she already knew what she needed to.

Dante's head swiveled toward his sister with a frown on his face. "What are you talking about, LeAnna?"

"We have a gift?" Marie perked up, her eyes wide with excited innocence. She then turned her inquisitive expression on her mother.

Cessily smiled fondly at her youngest. "Yes, Marie, we do. And I'm going to tell you all about it."

LeAnna moved toward the door, ushering the older brothers with her.

"No, stay, you three," Cessily said. "This will be new information to you as well. It seems I have been misled about the source of our power."

"Power?" Dante's eyebrow rose, his interest piqued. LeAnna, Rodney, and Isaiah paused inside the doorway to the bedroom, then trickled back in to find a place to sit or to lean against the back wall of logs.

"Yes, Dante, power. Our family has a special gift I want to tell you about. You are now old enough to know the truth, though I suspect you've been noticing strange occurrences already."

Dante nodded slowly, looking to each of his siblings. "I feel tingles sometimes at the base of my neck when most of you walk in from somewhere else. Though I don't feel it as much with Isaiah and not at all from Rodney. Why is that?"

Cessily nodded and took note of Rodney's face as his expression fell downcast. "None of that now, Rodney. You are not less than your brothers or sisters. You are a beautiful part of this family, just as your father is." A small smile lit Rodney's face as he accepted his mother's approval.

"I'll tell you a story. While you don't need all the details, it is the heart of the story I ask you to hear."

Marie folded her hands across her lap, her gaze filled with anticipation and intent upon her mother. The others leaned in, also expectant of what their mother was about to tell them.

"It began long ago in a country different from this one, taking place across the vast ocean in Europe. There was a family who had immense power—a strong and dangerous power. With power like that comes great responsibility to learn from it, to respect it, and to control it to use for good and protection. Unfortunately, as it has been chronicled throughout history, some of those with such power abused it, causing tremendous tragedy and pain. This story is not much different. But keep in mind that it can be." Cessily tapped Marie on the nose, then adjusted her position on the bed.

"What happened?" Dante asked, interest in his tone.

"Well, this particular family were called witch hunters," Cessily continued.

"Oh, this is rubbish, isn't it? It's just a tale for children," Dante huffed, disappointed with where the story was headed and crossing his arms in disapproval.

"No, dear one, this is not any tale I would tell my children unless absolutely necessary." Her eyes bored into her youngest son's, willing him to give her a chance.

"Let her finish, Dante," Marie scolded. "I want to hear the rest of the story!"

"Sorry, Mama, continue," Dante conceded.

"Thank you, son. Now where was I . . ."

"Witch hunters," Isaiah spoke up.

"Right. I don't believe they used this term back then, but perhaps they did. However, it was what they did—hunted witches, that is. It was a time in Europe when cries of witchcraft were becoming more prevalent, but not in any good ways, I'm afraid. The family took it upon themselves to seek out and sift through accusations of witches, deciding which were legitimate. You see, they could tell because of a particular sensation they could feel—a tingling that would travel up and down their arms."

Marie and Dante both held out their arms and looked down at their forearms simultaneously, stirring a chuckle and a snort from Rodney and Isaiah. Marie didn't care, but Dante shot them both a glare.

"Many of the witch hunters kept to themselves, not wanting to draw more attention to their oddities, but a select group of them took up the burden, feeling it was their duty and responsibility to shed light on any witches in the area. They figured they were given this ability, so they should use it for something."

"Makes sense," Dante said under his breath.

His mother gave him a reproachful look. "Except that they did not take into account the people they were accusing. People with families and children, people who didn't do anything harmful or against any laws of nature or men with their own gifts. Understand, there were witches who did terrible things with their magic and did go against nature—this was black magic, as we call it today."

"How could they tell the difference?" Marie asked wisely.

Cessily nodded, proud of her daughter. "When you feel black

magic, you know it deep inside." Cessily placed a hand at her stomach and one at her chest. "It's an overwhelming sensation. You feel ill and want to vomit. It can be so strong, you lose awareness of your surroundings and can even black out. The trick is to learn to remain alert and remove yourself from the situation."

"Mama, what happened back in Europe?" LeAnna steered the conversation back to the story. Cessily smiled, grateful for the redirect.

"Most of the family went into hiding. However, those who didn't agree went into a madness of sorts as they continued to hunt down all witches—not only black magic users, but even those who used their magic for good. This incited some of the European witch hunts that led to hangings and burnings of many innocent people —both human and witches alike. You see, the hunters were so charismatic in their dealings, even humans joined in the hunts, and they had no discernment as to who were true witches and who were not. It was a terrible time in our history." Cessily paused for a moment, lost in thought.

"How does this relate to us, Mama?" Rodney asked, though his expression revealed he might already know the answer.

"Well, I'm glad you asked. Many of those original witch hunters —the ones who wanted nothing to do with the hunts, but to live in peace and leave all that behind them—migrated here to this new country when ships began transporting people to and from the New World. I'm still absorbing all this information, as it is new to me as well." Cessily smiled, her eyes softening as she took in each of her beautiful children. She pulled her long hair around her shoulders to the front. "I have come to understand, through this journal recently given to me, some of those who migrated here from the old lands are ancestors of ours—a direct line to me, actually. You each have the hunting gene, some more than others. I have discovered it has not affected you all the same."

LeAnna frowned, genuinely engaged in the story for the first time. "Mama, you said our powers came as a gift from a nearby witch coven. I don't understand. Are you saying it wasn't a gift?"

"Yes. I mean it is a gift, but one we were born with and not given."

"I don't understand. What happened? How did you not know?" Isaiah, mature for his age at fifteen, asked.

"Sarah, the coven leader, told me the story, and it is reiterated here in this journal. Apparently, some of those early settlers went to the coven and asked for a spell to suppress their powers, so they might live in peace with their neighbors. You see, during those first years, quite a few covens emerged in close proximity as they fled farther away from Salem, and it would have driven our ancestors crazy with the constant overwhelming sensations."

"No one ever told you about it?" LeAnna asked.

"They put their heritage behind them in favor of living as the humans did and made a pact to not speak of it . . . except for the one member who kept this journal—I'm guessing behind the others' backs. It is not understood how the journal came to be in the possession of the witches, except for the way the author speaks of them; it sounds as if they were trusted friends."

"With the witches?" Dante grumbled.

"I, too, have trusted friends amongst the neighboring covens, especially Sarah's coven. My son, do not take the witches for granted and do not project the assumptions of our ancestors upon them. Every being, every creature, everyone has a place in this great wide world, and it's only getting wider as people continue moving out west. Soon the covens will be thinner and more spread apart, just as the hunters will be. There is balance to life. Don't ever forget that." Cessily addressed Dante specifically, but all her children as well.

Suddenly, Cessily clutched her chest as her breathing hitched, and she coughed into her other arm. The sound was alarming, as if her lungs were about to rise up out of her chest. The children took turns glancing around at the others, concern etched on their faces. LeAnna moved to kneel right at the side of Cessily's bed.

"Are you all right? What do you need?" She reached for the wet rag placed inside the blue and white porcelain bowl on the nightstand. Dipping it in the cool water, she then wrung it out and dabbed at her mother's forehead, now beaded with sweat.

"Children," Cessily rasped, her voice scratchy from the cough. "I am ill. I have been for quite some time, but it is now coming to the end. My time on this earth is almost over."

"No!" they shouted simultaneously. Marie scooted up closer to her mother's side and tucked herself into her as close as she dared, tears streaming down her face.

"It is my time. This is no way for me to live. But I want you to know all about your heritage—know, understand, and learn to control your power. You are not bound by the assumptions of what and who a witch hunter is. Redefine the term and explore new purposes for your gifts. You may come across others who won't understand you. Always be kind and generous. Go to the witches if you need help learning, as I did. Sarah will instruct you as she did me. After all, it was her mother and grandmother who helped our ancestors in the past."

"Can't they help you? Heal you?" Isaiah pleaded, tears in his eyes. Marie sniffled on the bed next to her mother.

"No, I'm afraid not. They do not interfere with the laws of nature when it is someone's time to go," Cessily said sadly.

"What? Didn't they wake up the hunter in you?" LeAnna asked, a frown creasing her brow.

"They have the power to heal you but refuse to? Maybe they did this to you? Did you think of that?" Dante asked, his arms crossed as he stood adamantly.

"No, they did no such thing. It is a long story, and I do not wish to spend my last moments with you sharing the how and why of my hunter side's awakening. When you are older, LeAnna can share it with you, but I have also added it to the end of this journal, so we will not forget who we are ever again. Learn who you are, but discover who you can be. Be reminded of the past, but write your own futures, each one of you." Cessily's voice grew weak, and her eyelids fluttered.

"Mama, don't go . . ." LeAnna's voice broke, and she laid her head on the quilts covering her mother's lap. Cessily loosely placed her hand on LeAnna's head and kissed the top of Marie's against her shoulder. Looking at each of her boys one by one in the eyes, she willed them to feel her heart.

"Be good. Help your father. He will need you. Grow strong and take care of each other. I love you always."

Cessily's eyes closed, and she did not reawaken.

CHAPTER 3

10 YEARS LATER

CENTRAL VIRGINIA ~ 1850

Twenty-year-old Marie sat cross-legged on a large boulder, enjoying the warm spring sun and noting the green sprouts of the newly planted crops emerging from their long winter's nap in the soil. Her grandparents, who had passed on when she was young, had built their beautiful log home set on acres and acres of land, on which they had made their money raising tobacco. Her father, Hank, had learned the trade of grape-growing from his side of the family, and he also grew a healthy stock of grapes for pressing into wine. Though Marie was of age, she and her siblings Rodney and Dante still lived at home with their father, while LeAnna and Isaiah had married and moved into smaller cabins on their property, to remain close.

Having taken her mother's role as ambassador to the neighboring witch coven, still led by her mother's old friend Sarah Stronghold, Marie would often take their excess vegetables to them as gifts of peace. None of it was required, but Marie felt compelled to do it. Additionally, Sarah's daughter, and successor as future coven leader, was Marie's best friend Rachael.

Rachael had trained with her mother for years, but still struggled to control her magic. Rachael's magic worked differently than her mom's—and most of the coven's, for that matter. She had a hard time doing things the way they had always been done in the name of tradition. Rachael had plenty of magic—Marie could feel her strength simply from the level of vibrations that would reverberate up her arms when Rachael would cast—it just wouldn't do what she wanted it to when she wanted it, such as at the command of her mother or during her training sessions, which were often.

Rachael and Marie had instantly hit it off when Marie brought a peace offering in the form of a large basket filled with vegetables and breads shortly after her mother, Cessily, had died. Young Marie felt it necessary to inform Sarah, since they had been friends, according to her mother. Marie had only seen the woman a couple times, though she didn't know she was a witch back then, not until her mama informed them all they were witch hunters. Marie and Rachael had been secretly inseparable ever since. Once LeAnna had let it slip in front of the boys who Marie's new friend was, they had given her a hard time, but none as hard as Dante. He couldn't believe her treachery of being friends with "those people who let Mama die," and he didn't let her forget it.

The winter—and ultimately year—after her mama's death had been the roughest that Marie and the rest of her family had ever faced. Especially her daddy. She had never seen him cry before that time. Her daddy was a big, strong man with broad shoulders, but he had a tender heart, and her mother's death had left a gaping hole —in not only his heart, but all of theirs.

Years later, Marie found herself reading once again the journal that enlightened and changed her and her siblings for the rest of their lives. The journal was ancient, but somehow still intact, even after all the years of reading material it had provided, for her especially. The others had moved on, but she read it over and over, sure there was more to their story, a deeper meaning and understanding of who they were as witch hunters. Her mother had talked about redefining and discovering who they could be anew, a dawning of a new era, and she was set on learning what that meant.

"I don't know if I'm expecting you to give me some kind of revelation or that the words of the pages and the heart behind whoever wrote in you will wear off on me, but I'm looking for some insight on how to keep control of my hunting drives without losing them completely," Marie said aloud to the book as she turned yet another page, then squinted up into the afternoon sun, allowing the warm rays to seep into her pores.

She just knew there had to be a way. So far, she had done pretty well, especially considering her best friend was a witch—nothing ruined a friendship like trying to kill your best friend. She had learned to limit her time with the entire coven; being around too many was near impossible at times. Marie found that knowing them as individuals and feeling the peaceful magic they performed helped. Sarah, the coven leader, would offer a temporary bandage of sorts when Marie planned to spend any length of time with the coven, to cushion the effects she experienced simply by being in their presence. As she grew older, however, the drive had gained in strength, and it was a constant battle to stay in control. Marie didn't even know what she would do if she did lose control, but that was a risk she definitely wasn't willing to allow. Too much was at stake.

A small white butterfly flitted across her peripheral vision, landing on an early flowering shrub and making Marie smile. The shape of the insect brought the cover of the book to mind. Marie closed the worn thick brown leather tome and ran her hand down the front. Inlaid within the leather was an intricately created design that reminded her of a butterfly or a cluster of small diamond-shaped stars, made out of latticed metalwork. It was the same symbol as the one etched on the spine, the same symbol marking every hunter's skin at birth—the hunter's mark. She ran her hand gingerly over the cool metal and what appeared to be some kind of locking mechanism.

"Why do you have a lock that doesn't appear to actually lock anything?" Marie wondered aloud, not for the first time. Opening it, she gently turned the first blank page to the next, and she began to read. The next hundred pages or so read like anyone's journal, recounting experiences and trials of the writer's time. In several places, the writing changed as the author changed—most likely, a descendant of the first. Each story, each obstacle they faced, described the pain they endured to control their hunting drives, mirroring her own struggle. Each author, at one point before their stories ended, spoke of finding the key or how the "key" showed itself to them in different ways than the last.

"But nobody explains what this key is or where to find it? That's not very instructional. How is this supposed to help me?"

"Talking to yourself again?" a male voice interrupted her. A tall and handsome man with broad, strong shoulders moved toward her with a lazy smile and a twinkle in his eye. The slight breeze picked up his blond hair and ruffled it the way Marie longed to do, sliding her fingertips through each wavy lock.

"I didn't think I was going to get to see you today, Judson!" Marie bounded off the rock, ran to him, and threw her arms around his neck just as he opened his arms wide enough to catch her with a twirl. She giggled as she always did upon seeing Judson after they had been apart. "I missed you."

"Ah, Marie, I missed you, too! I couldn't stand to not see you today. Are your brothers around?" Judson's gaze cautiously slid past her to the fields.

"No. I've been out here reading the journal Sarah gave my mother before she died."

Judson relaxed at the prospect of them having a few minutes

alone. The Blackstone boys did not like Judson hanging around Marie. They had made their point very clear years ago when Isaiah and Dante forbade her from seeing him or going near that "condemned hellhole of heathens," as they referred to the neighboring coven.

"Did you find out anything you hadn't seen the other hundred times you've read it?" Judson asked, his lip ticking up at the side in a teasing fashion.

Marie pulled at one of his suspender straps and let it go, snapping it back onto his chest.

"Hey! That hurts!" he whimpered, rubbing the painful spot.

"Serves you right, teasing me," she said flirtatiously while she patted her hand against his chest. She then leaned up on her tiptoes and kissed the underside of his chin before she stepped back to allow some thinking space. "Actually, I did find something I haven't truly examined yet."

"What's that?"

Marie held out the journal for him to see as her fingers traced over the metalwork. "Look at this shape, Jud. I thought at first it was a strange butterfly, but I see the diamond-shaped stars of the hunter mark."

Judson peered closely at the cover, nodding with a studied frown.

"And I think something is supposed to fit in inside here, but I don't know what. Mother never said anything about a key or a lock. Except it doesn't seem to lock anything, as we have obviously opened and read through it. Doesn't that seem odd to you?"

"It is odd, and it's an oddly familiar shape, though I am not sure where I've seen it other than the marking on the back of your neck. I've seen this in metal work." Judson frowned, thinking. "I'll figure it out. I just need it to come to me."

"It's time to go," Marie said unexpectedly.

Jusdon's head snapped up. "Your brothers?"

"I feel them coming closer. I'll come to you later tonight. Meet at our spot?" she asked, suddenly shy and biting her bottom lip.

"I wouldn't miss it." He leaned forward and kissed that bottom lip until she opened for him and allowed him full access to her mouth, groaning as she did.

Marie pulled back. "Tonight then. Now go, quickly."

Judson turned and loped into the brush and trees beyond their property, disappearing out of sight just in time.

"Marie? Where have you been?" Rodney called. "You were due at the house some time ago."

Her brothers all headed in her direction. Rodney, the only one of them human like their father, with dark hair and brown eyes, was the only brother usually sympathetic to her quest for peace with the witches. Isaiah, the eldest brother, looked most like father, but with sandy brown hair and flat blue eyes void of any spark of excitement or joy. Next to them stood Dante, who was closest to her in age, but furthest from the desires of her heart. With their father's hair but their mother's face, Dante was a fair blend with dark hair but bright blue eyes always calculating, always watching. They all awaited her response.

"Sorry, I got caught up reading over Mother's old journal again," she responded truthfully.

"Why do you bother with that old thing, Marie? If there was any information that would be helpful, you would have found it by now." Isaiah bent down to secure one of his laces on his worn work boots.

"I think I found something new this time!" Marie said, excited to share what she had found on the cover of the book. "Have any of you seen this shape anywhere in the house? Did Mother ever say anything about a key that went to this journal? I was young. I don't remember everything before she died." Her voice grew quiet. She knew they didn't like it when she brought up their mother, but it was time they discussed everything.

The brothers each looked at the cover of the journal, frowned, then shook their heads in answer to her question.

"Why are you pushing this, Marie?" Dante began with a cool tone that spoke to the end of his patience on this matter. He looked beyond her and out into the trees bordering their lands.

"I'm not *pushing* anything, Dante! I just believe there is more to learn about our hunter side, more to know in order to control it better and to find peace with our neighbors. Don't you want to know if there is another way?" With hands on her hips in defiance, she looked to each of them. Rodney looked away from her, the fear of his brothers' retribution if he agreed with her resident in his eyes. She knew they were hardest on him especially, being human and not quite like them.

Isaiah scoffed. "I don't really care, no. I have everything perfectly under control, as you should, too. Or perhaps you're just weaker than the rest of us."

Marie glared at Isaiah. He was her least favorite.

"Enough, Isaiah," Dante interfered. Though younger, he was somehow the dominant brother. "Marie is and will be by far stronger than you. She just needs to get her perspective and priorities back to *this* family."

"That's got to be hard for her to do when all she thinks about is ways to be at peace with the witches," LeAnna, her only sister, interjected, heading their way with a snide look on her face.

Marie glared even harder at LeAnna. Out of her entire family, LeAnna and her father were the only ones who knew her secret—and LeAnna only knew because she happened upon her and Judson once, having followed Marie at a distance.

"Why do you care so much, Marie?" Isaiah blurted now with anger.

"Because I do! It's the right thing to do. It's what Mother believed, don't you remember that?"

Marie glanced at Dante, who simply watched the interaction

with detached observation; however, a spark of knowledge flashed in his eyes.

"Why don't you just tell them and get it over with, Marie? They're going to find out one way or another." LeAnna hinted overtly that she would be the one to tell them otherwise.

"LeAnna! It is not your business to tell. You have ruined everything!" Marie shouted. Angry, fearful tears welled in her eyes.

LeAnna crossed her arms, bracing for what was to come, and raised an eyebrow. "No. You did, when you went off and married that heathen witch pretender!"

Shocked gasps reverberated throughout what felt like the entire world.

"You did what?" Dante seethed.

Marie crossed her own arms defiantly, staring her siblings down. "I married Judson Carter. In secret."

"Months ago," her sister supplied.

"Traitor," Marie shot back.

"No, Marie. You are the traitor," Dante whispered in a tone far worse than shouting, before he turned his back to her and left.

CHAPTER 4

$\mathcal{I}$n the shed, Dante, Isaiah, and LeAnna gathered weapons while Dante spewed his hatred for the witches. "We act now. It's time those evil-doers knew where they truly belong."

"You know I'm with you, but I'm curious about the source of your hatred—other than being a witch hunter," Isaiah asked, cleaning off a blade on the leather of his work boots.

Dante hung his head for only a brief moment, breathing heavily as if grasping the frail tendril of his sanity. "They killed Mother. Is there any other reason necessary?"

His words were burdened with the pain of the young boy within him and bound to the deeds of the man he was now—a man ready to avenge the only real love he had ever felt, a woman the witches had called "friend." A woman *they* could've helped, but chose not to.

"They haven't bothered us in some time, Dante. Maybe it's okay to simply ignore their existence for now," LeAnna said, as if she wasn't truly sure she believed what she said, but spoke more for the sake of saying it. Shrugging her shoulders, she went back to picking at her nails, unwilling to look Dante in the eye.

"We have suffered those witches too long, LeAnna. You are either with us on this or against us, like your sister you so easily outed." Dante's stare was fierce and unrelenting, and his determination pressed upon her until she nodded her head.

"I'm with you," she whispered, almost regretfully, and reached for a dagger on the wall before her. She spun away, toward the cracked open door, and walked out. "I'll be there. I need something from my cottage."

"We go at nightfall," Dante instructed, eyeing her as she left.

LeAnna stopped in the doorframe, half turned her head to acknowledge him, and nodded.

~

"Going somewhere?" a voice uttered from the side of the shed, hidden in the shadows from the fading sun.

LeAnna jumped, hand held over her heart. She caught her breath.

"Oh, Marie, you startled me!" she whispered, grabbing Marie's arm and tugging her to follow behind her.

Marie jerked her arm away, but continued to follow her sister. "I heard Dante. He can't do this."

"I don't like the witches and don't think we should assimilate with them, but I don't think they all deserve to die." LeAnna's eyes saddened, then frantic fear quickly took over, bubbling up in her eyes. She looked over her shoulder. In a hushed but hurried tone, she added, "You have to go. You have to warn them."

"Oh, I plan to. But why, LeAnna? Why did you tell them? You knew how they would react."

"I . . . I didn't think he would go this far. I'm truly sorry, Marie. I was jealous of your control and your devotion to living your own way." LeAnna lowered her head, ashamed and genuine.

Marie gently pulled her sister forward. She leaned in and kissed

25

the top of her sister's head. "I forgive you, but this is going to get bad. I have the feeling our family will never be the same after this night, and I want you to know forgiveness when you might not be able to offer it to yourself."

Marie turned and ran with all she had through their fields and into the forest, following the path to the secret place she and Judson had planned to meet, like they had multiple nights before this one.

～

"Marie, what's wrong?" Judson asked, his voice laced with panic at Marie's sudden and disheveled appearance.

She flung herself at him, wrapping her arms tightly around his neck, and held on as if her life depended on it. Sobbing uncontrollably, her words were incoherent as she tried to explain what had happened.

"Slow down. I can't understand you." Judson spoke calmly, as if to a frightened animal. Marie nodded quickly and inhaled several slow, deep breaths.

"We don't have time for this," she spoke between her breaths. "He's coming . . ."

"Who is coming? Where?"

"Dante . . . knows about us . . . not happy," she panted, still bringing her breathing under control.

Closing her eyes, she borrowed time she didn't have to collect her words. Marie gripped Judson's biceps as he held her steady, each arm bracing her shoulders. Her gaze found his, and she could see the resonance of their greatest fear coming to the forefront.

"Dante found out about us. He's beyond reasoning and planning to attack the coven tonight, after nightfall," she finally got out.

"We knew this day could come, Marie. It was a risk we took." Judson embraced her quickly, then pulled her back to see her face.

"The coven is strong. They can fight back, defend their homes, their lives."

His words were strong, but a current of uncertainty ran underneath.

"But do they want to? It could mean a lot of bloodshed, Judson. Dante has more than just his siblings. There are others—our mother's cousins, their children, and other hunters sympathetic to his argument against magic users, whether good or evil. I couldn't bear it if any of your family—my friends—got hurt or worse." Marie buried her face in her hands, her body racking with sobs once more.

"Shh . . . Marie, it will be okay . . . somehow." Judson tried to soothe her, but fell short.

"What do we do? We have to warn them!"

"Yes, we will warn them. I haven't had the chance to tell you yet . . . many of the coven have already left. We've heard of other covens heading west, seeking better lives—even talk of other supernaturals wanting to live in harmony together. I wanted to be able to approach you about it when there was time to really think if it was something you wanted or not. I mean, your family is all here, and I wouldn't ask you to leave them behind, but it might be an alternative . . ." Judson's face filled with uncertainty. He was unsure of her reaction.

"Judson . . ."

"If you don't want to leave, I'll stay behind. We'll find a way to be together. I know we can." The words fumbled out of his mouth before she was able to finish.

"Judson! I think that's brilliant. Get the witches all to leave, right away. I'll go home and pack. There's no way my family—well, Dante and Isaiah—would let me stay anyway. This might be our only chance to be together. It saddens me, but I feel in my heart it's the right thing to do. Make sure Rachael leaves and doesn't try to stay and be some martyr, please."

Judson answered by picking Marie up and twirling her around, as he favored doing. "I'll go right now and tell them. Go home and pack. It will be a long and arduous journey with many unknowns. Is it safe for you to go home?"

"I'll make sure of it. Dante wouldn't hurt me—at least I don't think he would. Please hurry. I'll meet you in one hour."

Judson pulled her close and took her mouth deeply, passionately, and desperately, as if he might not get another chance —for all they knew, he might not.

Marie pulled out of his embrace, knowing she would never leave his side if she didn't go now. Too much was at stake this night. She had to do what she could to make it right.

CHAPTER 5

"*Y*ou really love him, don't you?" Rodney asked as he stormed into Marie's room after she had burst through the house, racing to her space. He watched Marie frantically stuff things into a thick cloth bag with handles.

"I do. And I'm leaving with him, Rodney. What Dante is about to do is beyond what it means to be a witch hunter. I know it here." She placed her hand over her heart. Marie then stuffed her bag with some blouses and skirts, a couple cotton dresses, a wool coat and hat, and even a pair of trousers with suspenders she had stolen from one of her brothers long ago. Trousers were much more practical for working outside, and she didn't understand why women weren't supposed to wear them. She topped it off with some undergarments, including wool pantaloons.

"I agree, but I can't stand up to Dante. He can be crueler than you have ever seen." Rodney hung his head in shame and shifted his gaze toward her window.

Marie stopped rushing about the room and stopped in front of her brother. Her eyes held understanding and concern. "I know,

Rodney. Come with me," she whispered, suddenly excited with that thought. "You could! Come with me. You would be welcome."

A quick glimmer of something akin to hope flashed across Rodney's eyes, but he quickly shut it down. "I can't. What about Father? And the farm?"

"The others will still be here. Take what you can. Gather supplies . . . what kind, I have no idea . . . whatever you think. You're coming with me. You can start over, have any kind of life you want!" Marie's face lit up with the possibility for not only herself but for her brother, who would never hurt anyone purposefully.

Rodney's face broke with the slightest tip of a smile.

"Really? I could go?" he asked, as if the thought never occurred to him to leave the family and begin his own life—perhaps it hadn't. Their family had once been very close. Over the years, however, things had changed.

Marie nodded, then continued rushing about her room, gathering smaller items such as her brush, some family jewelry she had inherited from her mother, and of course, the family journal she was enraptured with.

"Okay. I'm going with you," Rodney announced more to himself and left her room swiftly, presumably to head toward his own room to pack.

"Hurry, Rodney. Less than one hour," she said, following him out of the room to make sure he heard. He waved, not even looking back at her.

Finally, she was packed with all she could think to take, including a few small family heirlooms, sewing and medicinal supplies, and some blankets. Running down to the kitchen, she opened the side door, then filled a small wooden cart with sacks of grains, flour, sugar, coffee, dried beans, rice, tea, and anything else she thought they would need. After all, she had no idea what their travels would be like. Marie felt giddy inside, like a young schoolgirl with her first crush. Her life was about to change forever, and she couldn't wait to start.

A loud crash came from outside, beyond one of the outbuildings. Shouts echoed to her ears, and her heart sank. Something was wrong. The sun was setting, and the fall of night was fast approaching. She didn't have time for whatever was happening. Marie raced toward the noise and practically smashed into Rodney, a bag strapped around his back. He, too, heard the shouting and dropped his bag next to her supplies. They took off together toward the angry cacophony of voices.

A sight she thought she would never see was laid out before her eyes. Isaiah, LeAnna, some of their cousins—from her mother's side, who only recently had the hunter awakened within them and barely held any control—and Dante all stood around, their father facing off with Dante in the middle. LeAnna looked torn, uncertain where her loyalties truly lay, but unfortunately, it appeared she leaned toward Dante.

"Oh no," Marie gasped with trepidation.

"Father," Rodney breathed in terror.

They both stopped at hearing the strong voice of their father. "Dante, this is wrong, son. You have to know that in your heart, if you still even have one. Your mother never wanted this for you or any of her children. She would turn over in her grave if she knew what you were considering."

Dante's eyes narrowed. He stood rigid and still, the calm before a storm. Without warning, without even an argument, Dante let the strength of his hunter surge to the surface as he hauled off and hit their father in the face, knocking him back into a pile of straw, which broke his fall as he landed on the ground. Stunned silence weighted the air around them all. Dante simply flexed his fist and turned from his father to finish whatever he had been interrupted doing in preparation for his attack. One thing Dante excelled at was planning and strategy. He never rushed into anything. Confidently, he must have felt he had time.

Dante's eyes darted to Marie, who caught his gaze as she ran toward their father. A glint of knowing sparked suspiciously in his eyes. Marie guessed he knew the distraction of helping their father would derail her from her immediate quest. Tears fell from her eyes, acknowledging the truth of what she didn't want to admit herself. She had lost Dante and most likely Isaiah as well. She was pretty sure she knew LeAnna would stay, but the separation still broke her heart. Growing up, they had always had differences and strong disagreements, but in the end, they were still siblings, still family, and they felt that connection. But no longer. Now she had to do what was right—what her mother would have wanted them to do.

"Father!" she cried as she and Rodney ran to him. Rodney helped their father up from the ground and led him back toward the main house. Hank cradled the shoulder he'd landed on. Marie placed her hand gently against his cheek, afraid she would hurt him. His left eye was already purple and so puffy, he could barely open it. Just below, his cheekbone was also blue and green, mottled with bumps—he looked as if he had the mumps. The sight tore at Marie's heart.

"I can't believe he went this far—to strike you, his own father!" Marie sobbed, leaning her head on his good shoulder.

"Let's get you in the house, Father," Rodney said as he took steps painfully slow.

Marie hesitated, just slightly, but enough that Rodney noticed. "You go, Marie. I'll tend to Father. Maybe I can meet you along the way," Rodney said, but they both knew the truth behind his words: if he didn't leave with her, he would never leave.

"Marie, you should go. It would be safer for you. I fear Dante will never stop. I will be fine," her father said through gritted teeth, his face barely able to function properly. "I will miss you, my daughter, and you, Rodney, my boy, but you both need to go."

"How did you know? I was coming to tell you," she asked, baffled by her father's easy acceptance.

"Your boy Judson is a good fella. He came to me awhile back and asked for my permission to ask for your hand, and between the two of us, we decided it should be kept secret. He also spoke of travelers going west, and the decision the witches had made to leave."

"I had no idea."

"Marie, you need to go now," Rodney urged as they slowly walked back to the house, passing their supplies and bags.

Marie's eyes lit with a sudden idea. "Father, you will come with us. After what happened, I don't trust your safety here anymore. The witches can offer something to heal you, I'm sure. Rodney, go pack him a bag quickly. Father, tell Rodney what to pack while I get a few more supplies. I will not take no for an answer."

Hank eyed his daughter and then his son with his good eye. He nodded tightly. "All right. I believe it would be what your mother would want. Although it tears me up to leave behind all our hard work and your family's legacy with this land and this house. We planted tobacco and then grapes, building a lucrative business, with our bare hands and sweat and labor. We've done a mighty fine job."

"Father, you can always rebuild, if you want. We'll find a new place to create a legacy that will hold strong and true to our beliefs for generations to come," Marie preached with passion. Hank gave her the tiniest smile and patted her arm.

"Let's go pack me a bag then, son, shall we? Marie, gather some of the planting seeds, my rifle, and gunpowder." Hank hobbled on his own, but moved slowly as Rodney stayed right at his side, arms out, prepared to steady him if needed.

She nodded and nervously wrung her hands together, knowing her time was growing too short, as darkness had fallen. "Perfect, then we will go."

"Go where?" Dante's voice came from the other end of the house. Marie froze.

"I don't want trouble, Dante. I'm leaving," she said calmly.

"I don't want you to leave. I want you to join me." Dante's voice was cool, almost too cool.

"I will not join you. It's not how I want to live."

"You would dishonor your heritage, the very essence of who you are, your power and all you could be, just to be with the pretend-witch who lives amongst them? To befriend those evil-doers over your own flesh and blood?" Dante stayed still as a statue, stoic in his stance and expression.

"I do not see it the same way, brother. I want to be free to live how I want, and I am not able to do that here." Marie remained calm, her voice steady and unprovoking.

"I see. Then I must follow what I believe and hope you will come to your senses and come back to us, to the rightful Blackstone family. Do not try to save your witches. You will be in the way." He turned to go, but snapped his head back her way, his eyes fierce with a raging fire of hatred. "I will not allow anyone to get in my way."

Marie's shoulders fell, and she breathed a sigh of relief at his absence. His presence was stronger than it had ever been before. She realized he had been holding his power back until that moment. The knowledge of that was crippling with the understanding of what he had to do to gain that power and further his control. He had to kill witches.

CHAPTER 6

$\mathcal{M}$oving fast was a high expectation with Hank injured and Rodney pushing the cart loaded down with supplies. They also gained a few extra tagalongs in the form of some of Marie's cousins who decided they didn't want to follow Dante and feared to stay. Marie finally reached the place she had intended to meet Judson. But Judson was nowhere to be found.

Screams rent the night air, and an urgency in the form of an electric jolt shot through Marie.

"Stay here and hide. I have to find Judson," Marie told Rodney and the rest with her.

"We can help. Let us come with you," the eldest of the teenagers who had joined them pleaded. He was tall and lanky with dark hair and fair skin. Most of her cousins did not have the hunter gene awakened, as they were not directly from her mother Cessily's line. However, if they committed an evil against the laws of nature, their hunter could awaken in a most unfriendly way—such as those who had bonded quickly with Dante and his quest against the witches.

"Fine, but stay together and watch out for Dante and the

others. I don't know what we're walking into." Marie paused and looked at each of them closely, examining them. "There are only a couple of you with your hunter awakened, correct?" Caroline, one of her cousins, and the boy, Michael, who had offered to help, both nodded. "Caroline, you are in charge of Uncle Hank, and Michael, you are in charge of the cart. I think if you have a focus, you may be able to control your hunting urges better. We head straight to the smithy to find Judson. Stay to the outskirts of the town. No matter what, stay clear of Dante. Am I understood?"

They all nodded and followed her the rest of the way into the town the Stronghold coven called home.

Nothing looked familiar. Marie paused just at the edge of the town, surveying all before her. Trees and homes were on fire, people were running and screaming from one end, and destruction and devastation were everywhere they looked. This was not the town she had been in just the other day. This was hell.

"Go that way," she yelled to Rodney, pointing her arm in the direction of the blacksmith's forge and hopefully to some sign of Judson. Stumbling over fallen debris and wreckage and breathing through pieces of material covering their faces against the smoke, they finally found the place Judson called home—the blacksmith's forge.

"Judson? Judson!" Marie called, sliding open the large barn door, then running into what really wasn't much different than a small barn with vertical planks of siding and small window slats up high. Pausing inside just long enough to let her eyes adjust to the dim interior, she searched frantically for Judson.

"He's not here, Marie," Rodney said, stating the obvious. His hands gripped each of his suspenders in an awkward manner.

"He has to be!" she shouted back, tears beginning to leak out her eyes, leaving tracks through her smoke-stained face. Angrily, she swiped those incessant tears away from her face.

"Marie?" a male voice whispered, coming from behind a hidden wall they hadn't seen. "Is that you?"

"Judson!" Marie ran to him, and he held his arms open to her.

"I couldn't get away to get to you. I'm sorry. I've been helping others to escape your brother's wrath and sneaking them into the bunker beneath the smithy," Judson explained. Strapped at his side was one of the daggers he had been working on.

Marie sighed a huge breath of relief, elated he was safe. "I was so worried," she whispered in his ear.

"As was I," he returned the whisper and kissed the soft skin just behind her ear.

A throat cleared behind them.

"What do you want us to do now?" her father Hank asked, breaking up their not-so-private moment. Marie blushed and pushed the hair out of her face that had fallen free of her clip as she stepped away from Judson. However, Judson gripped her wrist, not letting her far from his side. To his surprise, Hank gave him a slight nod of approval.

Marie looked to Judson. "How can we help?"

Judson examined each of those with Marie. "There are more of you than I thought, but we should manage just fine. There are several wagons prepared for us, but we can't leave now."

As if on cue, more screams pierced the night, followed by an explosion.

"This way to the bunker. Take what you can in case the worst should happen," he instructed, pointing beyond the wall just behind him. The others quickly followed his direction, down a narrow dirt tunnel that led below the forge into a cavern-like opening filled with other people.

Caroline and Michael paused at the top, clearly hesitant about going below to a confined space filled with witches. Marie gripped them each by their shoulders and turned them to face her. "You can do this. I believe in you completely. Stick together and focus on something simple, like helping someone. One of the witches should be able to offer a spell to help you, as they have for me when I come to visit."

They both took deep breaths and nodded, renewed by Marie's faith in them. Mission in mind, they quickly followed the others down.

"Judson, where's Rachael? And Sarah? Have you seen them? Did they get away?" Marie's voice took on a hint of panic and concern for her best friend.

Judson shook his head. "I haven't seen them. Sarah was waiting for everyone to leave before she left . . ."

"Of course, what else would a leader do?" Marie replied exasperatedly. She understood, but in that moment, she wished they had been selfish and got away. "I have to find them."

Determined, Marie turned to the barn door.

"Wait," Judson stopped her. "Take a weapon." He walked over to a wall with a lock on the edge of it. Judson slid a long skeleton key, strapped to his wrist with a piece of leather, into the lock. It popped and whirred with the sound of some mechanism giving way. Marie's jaw dropped.

"How did I not know about this?" She watched as the false wall split in two and flipped over with the help of some sort of clockwork pieces and cogs working together. With a puff of steam, the new side of the wall came to a halt, revealing multiple pieces of weaponry. Each was beautiful in its own right, with perfect metalwork, shining blades, and sharp edges. She gasped, eyeing all the weapons, from swords to daggers to maces and other types she didn't even know what to call.

"Pick one quickly," Judson instructed with a small smile, obviously pleased with her reaction.

"I'm not surprised, but did you make these?" she asked with wonder.

"I did."

"They're beautiful, Judson, really. Pick one for me?"

Judson reached forward and selected a slim dagger with a blackened handle, leading up to a darkened silver hilt covered with an elaborate design made of intricate metalwork. Marie's eyes grew wide, and her mouth opened in awe, ticking up at the sides to reveal a pleased smile.

She clapped her hands together and nodded. "It's perfect!"

Judson smiled. "Let's go."

She placed her hand on his arm to stay his movement. "No, I'm going alone. It's not safe, especially for you. I can move faster with my hunter speed if I don't worry about you keeping up with me. Don't be offended, Judson. It's just the way it needs to be. You have a job to do here. Keep them safe." She pointed to the bunker behind the wall.

"I'm not offended. I've known all along who you are and what you are capable of. I believe in you and will keep your family and mine safe. Just hurry and be careful." He kissed her on the tip of her nose and moved away, allowing her to go and do what she needed to do, trusting she was capable to achieve it and come back to him.

Marie did not tarry, but gingerly tiptoed out into the dark night lit only by the fires still blazing in some structures. As the night burned on, the flames began to dwindle. Though she didn't need the light because of her excellent hunter's vision, the fires provided extra shadows, which helped to conceal her. She lunged from structure to tree and then from tree to alternate structures, using whatever was left standing to help shield her. Voices rang out in the distance, hoots and hollers that she could identify as some of her relatives—it broke her heart to think of what they could still be doing to any witch they found alive.

Finally arriving at the Stronghold house, Marie dashed in the back door, which was hanging askew, off its hinges. Glass was shattered on the wooden planked floor. At the least, a struggle had happened, but what else, she couldn't determine.

"Sarah?" she dared whisper when the house was otherwise silent. Marie tiptoed through each room. "Rachael?"

Marie stopped. The sound of a boot scuffing on wood caused her to pause. Straining, she listened for which direction to go. Again off to her right, from a small darkened closet, she heard stifled sobs.

"Sarah? Rachael?" she tried again.

"Marie?" a broken voice whispered back. The door slowly opened to reveal Rachael, her hair matted and disheveled, her eyes red and swollen from crying, and cradled on her lap was her mother's head.

"Oh, Rachael," Marie mourned for her. Sarah obviously was dead, with her neck at an odd angle and her eyes open but unseeing. Marie moved slowly forward and gripped Rachael's hand while she gently closed the lids of Sarah's eyes.

"It's time to go, Rachael. They could come back," Marie quietly prodded.

Rachael shook her head adamantly. "No, no, no, I can't leave her. She died protecting me and others. I can't leave her here." She broke and sobbed so violently, her shoulders shook.

"Rachael, don't let her sacrifice be in vain. She protected you so you could lead her people . . . your people, the Stronghold Coven. You have to come with me now." Marie pushed her friend more than she wanted to. She wanted nothing more than to let her grieve and bury her mother in the place of their home, but it couldn't happen. Tears silently flowed down Marie's face as she helped pull her best friend away from her mother, away from every happy moment of her childhood and her home into an unknown and uncertain future.

Sadly and quietly, they made their way back to the forge and into the hidden bunker unseen.

THE NEXT MORNING, just as dawn approached, Marie stirred everyone who had finally and safely fallen asleep. Judson returned to the bunker after having scoped out topside, accompanied by several other men who hadn't been with them the night before.

"It's safe to go, but we need to go now. The wagons are waiting for us just outside. We need to put some distance behind us before next nightfall," Judson urged as he helped others gather their items. "These men are drivers who will be traveling with us. They brought the wagons."

One by one, they emerged from the smithy and out into the rising sun. The sight that greeted them was one that would forever be etched in their hearts and memories. Homes destroyed. Smoke still rising from the dying coals. Bodies of those unfortunate to have not found safety in time. Pure devastation. Judson helped by ushering them along into the wagons, not to linger, not to stare. Everyone moved somberly, and quietly they loaded all they had left into the multiple covered wagons pulled by two horses each. One wagon was devoted simply to crates and sacks of supplies as well as personal belongings. Cries were heard, but no one spoke until the last was loaded.

Marie reached for Rachael's hand before they loaded and gave Rachael an encouraging nod to speak to her people.

"Say goodbye, for this is the last we will see of this place. We move forward into the unknown, into the light of a new dawn, untainted by the evil of our past, into a future with new possibilities for us. For we are the Stronghold witches traveling with friends, and we will be strong." Rachael offered Marie a small smile, looking every bit the leader her mother always knew she could be. Marie couldn't have been more proud of her friend, knowing the pain she experienced underneath it all. "Many could point fingers and hope to blame and seek revenge upon those who we call friends because of their relations' sins, but know this: as of this very moment, they are under coven protection and considered ours."

Rachael stared each and every one of her people in the eyes to ensure they understood her message—mess with Marie and they mess with her. Marie's heart warmed while at the same time it broke, knowing what happened to them was her family's fault.

"For what it is worth, I am not my siblings, and my heart breaks alongside yours. I am truly sorry for what has befallen you and yours." Marie bowed her head, hoping they heard the authenticity in her words. Judson came to her side and laced his fingers within hers and kissed her temple.

"Time to go!" Judson announced as he helped Marie up into their wagon right after Rachael. The drivers flicked their wrists, jostling the reins of the horses, and off they went, putting the darkness of the town and the rising light of the day behind them as they traveled west.

CHAPTER 7

ARKANSAS ~ SUMMER 1851

*D*ays on the wagon trail were monotonous at best; one, two, three days soon turned into weeks. Sometimes they stopped only for one night, but other stops turned into settling for several days—even weeks and months—at a time, enough to give their backsides as well as the horses a break. Each stop only stoked the desire within their souls to continue west.

"Judson?" Marie asked one night as they sat around the fire, cooking a rabbit stew. He looked up lovingly at her, and she felt heat crawl up her chest. The man had a way of turning her insides into mush with a single look. "How will we know when we reach the place to be our new home? It seems we have been traveling for so long already."

The wagons were circled up around them, creating a barricade from the wind, allowing their fire to thrive in its shelter, and protecting them all from the elements and other dangers. Around the fire, they had placed several old logs to use as benches. Sitting upon them were those traveling with Marie and Judson: her brother Rodney, her father Hank, Caroline and Michael, and some of the other tagalongs they had adopted, as well as a few of the witches, who huddled next to Rachael. The days were quite warm to travel, but the evenings were chilling with early autumn breezes. The rolling green hills were beautiful during the day, and at night, they set the backdrop for the night's glory to unfold above them.

Roasting a piece of rabbit on a stick, Judson methodically rotated it for an even cook as if it was second nature to him.

"We will follow our hearts and our intuition." Judson patted his heart then his head. Marie glanced at Rachael, who nodded at his statement.

"And what of the rest of the Stronghold coven who left before Dante struck?" Marie asked hesitantly.

"We have several items of theirs to help locate them on the journey. We will find them," Rachael answered confidently.

Marie looked behind them in the opposite direction from the wagons and took note of the specialized tents they were given by the witches. Each tent was equipped with metal rods, which unfolded in segments, connecting together to provide a structure similar to teepees, then surrounded by thick leather stitched together to create "walls." On the outsides, where each end of the leather met, a large clasp held them together; the mechanism reminded Marie of the inside of a clock. When one pulled the lever, it made a ticking sound and then a click, which released the hook on the opposite end of the leather, allowing one to enter the tent and then reconnect it on the inside, even lock it for the semblance of privacy.

In the distance, a coyote howled, and a shiver ran up Marie's spine.

"I wonder where Dante and the others are?" she whispered for only Judson's ears. "Do you think they are looking for us?"

"I pray they are not," was his only reply.

"Many times while we've been traveling or after we stop, sometimes I get the faintest feeling of another hunter or that we're being watched. We can't let our guard down where he is concerned."

"Tonight, let's have Rachael and a couple of the others do an extra protective spell around the campsites," Judson suggested.

Marie nodded her agreement. "I'll ask her after dinner."

~

JUST AS DINNER HAD ENDED, one of the drivers, Butch, pulled out a well-loved five-stringed guitar and began to softly strum. Several people gathered around him and the fire to listen to the melodic tune as it floated up to the glittering dark sky above. Some men carved shapes and designs into sticks and pieces of wood to pass the time, a few of the women worked on hand-stitching pieces of fabric together to create more blankets for the coming cold, and Judson tinkered on some delicate metalwork inside his tent. Marie reached for Rachael's hand and pulled her over near one of the wagons for a semi-private conversation.

"How are you doing since . . . ?" Marie asked cautiously, concerned for her friend. Rachael was usually full of life and joy, but since they'd left and her mother had died along with many others from her coven, she had grown sullen and quiet.

"I'm making do, Marie." She sighed and gave her friend a small sad smile. Marie squeezed her hand. "I know the coven needs me, so I'm trying to get my heart and my head figured out."

"Give yourself time, Rach. You've all been through a lot, and your coven is dealing with it all still, as well."

"I know." Rachael gazed back at the fire, toward the remainder of her coven who hadn't left before Dante struck, and sighed again, shifting her gaze to her shoes. "I don't think they are going to accept me like they did my mom. My magic has always been a little different. They humored me while Mother was training me, but now . . . I'm not so sure." Rachael shrugged dejectedly.

"That's not true. They will love you. Right now, they're watching you to see how you respond to this tragedy, to see if you're strong enough to lead them—which you are, you just don't know it yet."

Rachael let out a brief laugh of disbelief.

"You are going to lead them into their destiny, and they will respect you for it," Marie continued, unfazed by Rachael's sarcastic sound.

"I don't know about that, but thanks, Marie. I appreciate you trying." Rachael gave Marie a quick hug.

"Before you go back to the fire," Marie started, "I think I've felt hunters." She held up her hands in a placating gesture. "Before you panic, whoever it is is not close, and I felt it a ways back. But just in case, Judson and I thought it best to ask if you can add an extra layer of protection tonight when you work your spells."

With hands on her hips and her head cocked to the side, Rachael raised a brow in attitude. "First of all, I have never panicked on you. Secondly, I have always known being your friend came with risks and have accepted them wholeheartedly, just as you have accepted my coven."

"There's my Rachael back." Marie giggled.

"But yes, I will add to the spell tonight. I'm even going to bring in some of the other witches to help." She paused, uncertain her decision was right after what they had been through. "Yes, that's what I will do. I am not going to hide things from them. They knew traveling would have its risks, and if we are to be a strong team, we need to be honest and work together." Rachael nodded decisively.

"Good plan," Marie agreed. "Thank you."

"No problem." Rachael hesitated, then added, "What do you think of the new men who joined us at our last stop?"

Marie frowned, then remembered. "Do you mean the Ahusaka brothers, the native shifters?"

"Yes, I haven't been around many shifters before. Mother had a few contacts who were wolf shifters, but their magic felt different than the brothers' magic does. They keep pretty much to themselves. Do you think we can trust them?"

"I haven't had many dealings with them either, but there is kindness in their eyes. I think we can," Marie answered. "Plus they're easy on the eyes, don't you think?"

"I suppose so, though I haven't noticed much," Rachael said, pretending to be haughty. But Marie knew if it weren't so dark, she would see a blush creeping up her friend's neck.

"Well, I'm not looking, but if I were, I think they are quite nice to notice."

Rachael giggled under her breath, knowing what her friend was after. "Well, I'll let you know if I do—notice that is."

"Sounds like a plan. Let's get back to the evening festivities. I need to check on Judson."

"I saw him enter your tent. I bet he'd allow you to observe how nice he is to notice," Rachael said in a teasing manner.

Marie laughed. "You need to work on your suggestive phrases. That could have been so much better."

Rachael laughed in return, then looped her arm through Marie's as they walked back to the group, sauntering with lighter steps than they had started with.

MARIE WOKE in the morning to find the sleep sack next to her empty. She stretched her body and felt it pull deliciously in places that made her ache for Judson again and again. He was her match in every way, and she couldn't imagine her life without him in it, which made his absence even more of a disappointment this morning.

She rose to find him speaking with a small group of men from their camp—a mixture of witches, the Ahusaka brothers, her father Hank, and the drivers of their wagons.

"Now what is going on?" Marie said to herself as she fastened their tent entrance back up, then headed to the group.

Smoke still drifted from the mostly burnt logs left over from the fire the night before, lifting into the rising dawn of the chilled morning. She could hear others stirring in their tents, preparing to come out to begin chores for breakfast. They had discovered the easiest way to work with everyone was to split chores and rotate them, so everyone pitched in and no one felt burdened with the bulk of responsibilities.

"Morning, everyone," Marie chirped, joining the group just as Rachael joined from the opposite side. The sun was just barely peeking above the plateau and the sounds of the nearby gurgling creek set the stage for a lovely day. Unfortunately, she had a feeling their meeting was anything but lovely. "What's going on? We haven't even had coffee yet."

Judson reached for her and pulled her to his side, tenderly kissing her temple. "Morning," he whispered in her ear, causing her to giggle before remembering they had an audience, and then she blushed.

"Do not be ashamed of your love," the older of the Ahusaka brothers, Alo, admonished. "It is always a joy to find love. It brings hope to all here." He gestured out toward the cluster of tents.

"Thank you." Judson acknowledged him with a nod.

"You are welcome, Atsidi," he returned with a slight incline of his head. Atsidi, Judson and Marie had learned, was their word for a blacksmith, and he recognized Judson as such.

"One of the brothers spotted a group traveling north of us," one of the drivers said, changing the subject.

"Is it the group we are hoping to meet up with? The other Stronghold witches?" Rachael asked, jumping in the conversation. They all turned to her as if just noticing she had joined them. Ahote, the youngest of the brothers, kept his gaze on her longer than the rest of the group as the driver answered her question.

"No, we do not believe it is."

Cetanwakuwa, the middle brother, confirmed his belief. "Alo felt darkness around them."

The Ahusaka brothers had explained when they first arrived that they were bird shifters—hawks to be precise. Each had additional gifts in addition to the shifting ability. Alo was the spiritual guide, a shaman to some. Ahote was a wanderer, but would argue it was his nature and not a gift at all. Cetanwakuwa was a fighter, and they called him the "attacking hawk" when speaking of him.

"Are we threatened by this group? Do we need to move on?" Marie asked.

"That's what we were discussing, whether it was time to move or if we should hold still and wait for them to pass farther away from our route," Judson explained.

"Could it be Dante? I don't think I could feel him that far away."

Judson and Marie had explained the situation, to those not aware, of Dante and the rogue hunters. Alo shook his head, his long black hair falling in front of his face as he did so.

"It does not feel like you." He turned his head toward Rachael. "It feels like you—magic users—but it is dark and harmful," he elaborated.

"Okay, so we've got some black magic users, dark witches, on our trail . . . literally. The question is, do they know we are here?" Marie shuddered at the thought.

CHAPTER 8

*A*fter much debate, the group decided to stay for a little longer. The motion of the caravans and the dust they kicked up during the day ultimately could have been more of a beacon announcing "come to us, we're over here" than they wanted. Lying low potentially could provide more protection as long as the dark witches kept on their current traveling path. After breakfast, they doused the fires, hoping to rid the sky of the smoke announcing their presence, and no one was allowed to make loud noises or play music. Perhaps they were overreacting, but they didn't want to take any chances of stirring up trouble.

"This is not ideal," Rachael complained as she and Marie took buckets down to the stream. They wandered a short walk through a forested area that brought Marie a smile; the air was invigorating. She hoped where they ended up settling would have beautiful scenery and flowing water even better than this place.

"No, it's not. But they were right—we're not ready for any kind of attack," Marie said with frustration. "We have witches and hunters and hawks . . . we should be prepared to face anything that might come our way. We should not cower in fear and hide, but at the same time, I understand. We have young ones with us too, and we don't need the trouble right now."

Dipping the buckets into the cool, shallow stream, they filled them.

"Why don't you train them then? Get them ready?" Rachael asked innocently.

"Me? What about you? You can work with the witches to come up with defensive and offensive spells, if necessary."

Rachael backed off. "Touché. They won't listen to me yet. I can feel they're not ready."

"Maybe you need to tell them that they're ready. Did you think of that? You can't coddle them. This is not the time or place for that. They will have time to nurse their scars when we settle, but not now."

Rachael sighed. "You're probably right. I'll come up with a list of spells and see how that goes over."

"Good girl!" Marie flicked a small splash of water at her friend. Rachael sucked in a deep, harsh breath.

"That is so cold!" Rachael retaliated with a slightly larger splash at Marie, who giggled and grabbed her bucket and ran back to camp, away from her friend who followed behind.

∽

AFTER NIGHTFALL, the camp was quiet as everyone retired to their tents. Marie tossed fitfully and turned in her sleep sack while Judson slept soundly beside her. Something pulled at her subconscious, an itching . . . an unpleasant feeling deep in the pit of her stomach she hadn't felt before, but had wondered about ever since she first read her ancestors' journal. Quietly, Marie slipped her traveling dress and her boots on, but left them unlaced, grabbed her shawl, and slipped out of their tent. Just enough chill in the night air had her wrapping herself with the wool shawl she was now grateful to have grabbed.

Marie tiptoed her way through the camp and around the wagons until she was able to peer into the dark night and the vast expanse of dirt laid out around them. Not much could be seen except the amazing array of twinkling stars against the black backdrop of the night sky and the occasional firefly still buzzing about before it retired for the night. The sight took her breath away each and every time she had the privilege of seeing it. Marie inhaled deeply and slowly, calming her nerves. Her intent wasn't even clear to her, but she knew the sick feeling in her stomach had something to do with the band of witches traveling parallel to them. She just needed to know what they were up to.

Stepping beyond the shelter of their campsite, heading toward an outcropping of tall boulders, she stopped dead in her tracks when a tall shadow emerged from the tree line not far from her.

"Going somewhere in the night, miss?" a deep male voice asked with somewhat broken-sounding English. "It is dangerous out there. Wild animals and more."

Marie's breath caught in her throat, and her heart pounded so hard it was about to burst from her rib cage. Not until the man stepped away from the shelter of the trees and into the glow of the moonlight was she able to recognize which of the Ahusaka brothers he was.

"Oh, Alo, you frightened me," Marie breathed heavily, placing her hand upon her heart as she attempted to catch her breath.

"Apologies, ma'am." Alo tipped his head toward her, but didn't move any closer. An awkward silence descended between them. He didn't press her any further, but she felt she owed him an explanation to answer his first question. Knowing Alo the little she did, he probably already had an idea of where she was off to. He had a way about him that suggested he knew much more than he let on about everyone and everything. It was slightly unnerving, but he had never done anything to suggest he was a danger to their group; quite the contrary, in fact.

"I have a strange feeling. I believe it's related to the other travelers you spotted earlier," she admitted freely.

Alo nodded thoughtfully. "With your gifts, I can understand. You cannot go out there on your own. I gave my word to your Atsidi to watch over this camp and you. I will not allow it on my watch."

Slightly deflated and slightly relieved at not having to sneak around, Marie nodded with understanding.

"I won't get you in trouble, Alo. It just bothers me I don't understand what it is I'm feeling yet." Marie rubbed one forearm, then the other.

"Trust your instincts, and they will guide you," Alo directed in a voice full of wisdom. His brothers had referred to him as a shaman or a spiritual guide, so she took his instruction to heart.

"Thank you. Good night," Marie said as she turned and went back to her tent. She couldn't shake the feeling that something bad was happening, but somehow believing in herself allowed it to move to the background of her mind for the rest of the night.

CHAPTER 9

*D*ays had passed with much the same routine as the ones before, and no trouble had arisen from the band of witches who traveled parallel to where they were camped. Rachael practiced her magic at the edge of their campsite, between large boulders and the stream to shield her and give her privacy. However, Marie couldn't help notice a certain Ahusaka brother who watched from higher up on the cliff of one of the plateaus, overlooking where she practiced unaware. Ahote seemed to study Rachael, and perhaps he was simply curious in a witch's magic, but Marie saw something much deeper in his eyes.

"Judson?"

"Hmm?" Judson didn't look up from the work table he had crafted out of two barrels and a fallen log he had split on both sides to make flat for his use. Marie moved closer to him to inspect what he worked on.

"Have you noticed how Ahote watches Rachael? I think he might have feelings for her." Marie tested her theory on him. Judson glanced up at Marie, and she nodded to where Ahote sat curiously on the cliff. Judson's gaze followed hers.

"Perhaps he does. Do you have thoughts against that?" he asked.

"No, just wondered what you think. If she likes him in return, I see no harm. I just care for her and her well-being."

"I know you do, as do I." Judson turned back to his project, unconcerned.

"What are you working on so intently?" Marie crossed her arms and bent forward to look closer.

Judson's face turned toward Marie. He was lit up like a star, his smile reaching his eyes—the excitement he showed couldn't be contained. "It's for you! Well, I actually already gave it to you, but I've refinished it."

"What is it?" Her own excitement mirrored his as she bounced on her toes and clapped her hands.

Reverently, Judson held out his flattened palms, where his pet project these last days rested—a small dagger, the edges blackened within the blacksmith's fire. The shiny blade held an inscription in Latin, and intricate metalwork decorated the front of the hilt. Marie gasped.

"It's the dagger you gave me before we left. You fixed the mangled metalwork. Oh! It's the same design from my family journal! How did you replicate it?" Marie asked in shock and a bit of awe.

Judson's face held a sheepish expression he rarely showed, and he hesitated.

"What? What is it, Jud?"

"I wanted to tell you earlier, but I wanted to see if I could remake it first. My mother gave it to me before she left for the northern coven where her relatives lived. She said it had come to her from Sarah's mother, who had asked her to keep it safe and hidden. My mother told me it had belonged to hunters who had given it to her as a symbol of their vow to protect and not hunt the coven."

Marie's eyes grew wide as she listened to Judson's tale, even though they refused to leave the dagger he had placed into her own hands.

"I hadn't thought much more about it, other than it being an interesting dagger I was drawn to, but when I saw the design on your journal, I knew they were connected—items in partnership. It was in rough shape—some of the metal pieces were bent out of shape or broken, the blade had dulled over time, and it needed care and attention. I gave it some," he said proudly and puffed out his chest.

"Indeed you did. It's beautiful. This colorless stone in the center is amazing and truly unique. What does the phrasing mean?" She pointed to the words inscribed horizontally on the blade from tip to hilt.

"*Elige tibi*. It means 'Choose yourself,'" he translated.

"That's amazing. Thank you!" Marie reached up and pulled him closer to her by placing her hand behind his neck. She leaned her forehead against his and simply rested against him, sharing the air between them. "I love it, and I love you."

Then she kissed him softly and tenderly on the lips, but before he could take the kiss deeper, the sound of a hawk's cry pierced the sky, and they startled apart.

"It's Cetanwakuwa. That's a warning someone is approaching our camp," Judson explained as he grabbed Marie's hand and pulled her after him. "Hold onto your dagger, Marie. We don't know what kind of danger approaches."

Judson and Marie reached the edge of the wagon circle. Men stood around, hoping for a nonchalant appearance, but each one held a rifle or another weapon—some more inconspicuous than others—from Judson's weapons cache that he had brought with them. Marie's brother Rodney and her father Hank were among them, looking just as fierce, comfortably holding their rifles as any with metal weapons.

"What's the trouble?" Judson asked the men out front.

"Wagon headed this way," Marie's cousin, Michael, stated, signaling off in the distance just beyond the gathering of rocks standing as pillars.

A cloud of dust kicked up, announcing the visitor before the wagon even came into view. It didn't move fast, but clipped along at a steady pace, allowing them a few minutes to breathe and prepare before their guest arrived. Several of the witches strategically arranged themselves behind the wagons and sent the younger ones into one of the tents with an extra protection spell. The male witches were less common than the women from the Stronghold coven, but the ones who were skilled in their magic hid in a few of the covered wagons, watching carefully. Presenting a fairly large welcome party, Marie stood just behind a large wagon wheel, waiting to get a read on who approached them. She didn't have offensive powers like the witches, but what she did have she would use if the time came.

"It comes," Ahote said from where he leaned against one of the large wagon wheels off to the side from everyone else. He crossed his legs at his ankles and folded his arms, but kept his head up and his eyes trained on the approaching wagon.

Marie shook her arm with the familiar tingling she would get when visiting the coven.

"Witch," she whispered.

The wagon slowed to a stop not far from where they all stood. The wagon itself—pulled by only one horse—was smaller than one of their traveling ones and shaped more like a rectangle with cut outs for windows and a railing on the back of a platform from which stairs could be pulled down. On the side of the box were words in a fancy script, advertising tonics, potions, lotions, and spells. It appeared they were dealing with a traveling salesman looking for his next pitch.

However, the man in the driver's seat looked like anything but a salesman. Slumped over, he barely held the reins for the horses. His hair was disheveled and matted. The clothing he wore was tattered and singed. As Alo approached, the horse reared back, a hint of madness in his eyes and foaming at the mouth.

"Whoa!" Alo called to the beast. He then spoke in a soothing tone in his own language, and the horse slowly calmed down. Alo grabbed the reins and pulled the horse to a stop.

Judson and Rodney were the first to reach the wagon while others raised their rifles, ready for anything.

"Is he okay?" Marie shouted.

Most couldn't hear what the men were saying, but Marie heard them trying to get information from the man, who appeared to be barely conscious. What she did hear from his garbled words was that his camp had been attacked in the night. He barely got away and didn't know if any of his people were alive. He came looking for help. Marie ran up to the wagon next to Judson.

"Who attacked you? Do you know?" she asked with a slight panic in her tone. Fear gripped her heart.

The man raised his head and looked at Marie. His eyes widened and his face flinched.

"You. His eyes looked like yours do," the man said with fear in his voice. He pointed a shaking finger in her face. "You're one of them, aren't you? You're a witch hunter!"

Marie gasped and stumbled back to the ground, away from the man and the wagon. Her fear was realized: Dante. Dante had attacked them. Guilt gripped her heart. She wondered, if she had been able to follow her gut feeling the other night, whether she could have warned those witches.

"You're safe now." Rodney tried to soothe the man.

"Not safe. You have a hunter in your camp," the man said with a sudden renewed energy as he sat up and gripped the reins out of Rodney's hands. "I will save myself."

The hawk overhead screeched once more and dove from high in

the sky down toward the wagon, now pulling out from their camp. The man shouted at the top of his lungs, "They will come for you, hunter! And take out everyone with you, you and all your abominations! We won't let more of our people fall to your kind again."

The hawk dive-bombed the driver, attacking as he chased him away from the camp.

"Come back, Cetan," Alo whispered to his brother as if he could hear him all the way up in the sky. Maybe he could, because the hawk stopped attacking and circled back toward the camp.

Marie and the entire camp stood in stunned silence. Her brother most likely killed that other band of witches—good or bad witches, she didn't wish her brother's wrath upon anyone.

CHAPTER 10

"*I* think it might be time to discuss moving on to a new location," Rachael brought up later that day when they were gathered around the fire, preparing the evening meal.

Marie knew she needed to be grateful for fresh food while they were able to find it, but she was tired of the fish from the stream, the rabbit she had to pick out buckshot from, for fear of cracking her teeth, and the random bits of fur clinging to the occasional elk. Once they were back on the trail, they would only have available the breads they had been making while camped and the beans, rice, and jerked meats that wouldn't spoil along the way.

"I think you might be right," Marie responded reluctantly.

"We were going to wait a few days longer, but it won't make much difference." Judson shrugged.

"I'm not excited about getting back in the wagons, but I feel something bad might happen if we don't," Michael said, fidgeting uncharacteristically with his hands.

"I agree," Marie said with certainty. "That man in the wagon said they would come for us, but he also said he wouldn't allow for more of their people to fall to my kind—the hunters. Dante. He had to have been speaking of my brother, Dante. Which means he's out there somewhere and perhaps not far from us. I don't want to risk any of you by staying in one place too long."

Judson reached for her hand and laced his fingers with hers. She squeezed his in return.

"I think we all echo that sentiment. Sounds like it's time to pack up," Hank said with a discouraged tone that caused them all to glance his way. He nodded decidedly despite his tone, but added a small smile. Marie knew anytime Dante was brought up, her father felt like he had failed somehow. She went over and leaned against her father's healed shoulder and allowed him to wrap his arm around her own.

"He made his choices, Father."

"I know, but it doesn't make it any easier for a parent," he said softly.

"Then it's settled," said Butch, one of the drivers of the lead wagon, to all present. He was a no-nonsense man in his late sixties with skin leathered by time and the great outdoors. Butch had traveled with the wagons on several different occasions and knew the route better than anyone with them, so he called the shots when it came to traveling. His plan was to get them west to their destination, then head back east to start another wagon train all over again. His life was the trails. Butch wasn't bothered by the witches and other supernaturals who traveled with them. He himself was a bit of a mystery, but was indeed not wholly human. Then, in a much louder voice perfect for herding cattle, he yelled, "Round 'em up! We leave at daybreak!"

~

ROLLING hills of green dotted with hints of gold, separated by rivers and lakes, was a landscape worthy of traveling through. After being on the trail for a couple days with only brief stops, trying to gain as much ground as the caravan could, they had reached the Ozark Mountains, where they needed to turn north to reach Independence, Missouri.

"Judson, how far out are we from Independence?" Marie asked as their wagon bumped along a rugged section of the trail. She and Judson had opted to drive one of the wagons for the day, which allowed them some time to themselves, at least until someone came up and joined them from the back.

"A couple days still, I believe. My navigation skills with the landmarks and stars is not near what Butch's ability is. I think he has some kind of magic for it, if you ask me."

"How long will we stay in Independence?"

"It will depend on whether the others from the coven are there or we have to wait on them. It was their plan to reach that far. It will also depend on our route and where we want to spend the winter. It could be quite dangerous to travel near the Rocky Mountains during the peak of winter. Plus, there are supplies in Independence, so we will take some time and make sure we have enough gunpowder, food, and supplies, and most likely trade some of the mules and horses in for oxen."

Marie's forehead scrunched as she thought through his words. "Why would we want oxen instead of horses? Aren't they slower?"

"Yes, but there have been rumors of the Comanches and Apaches attacking those traveling through parts of those areas. The trail has been protected by the government, but we don't want to risk it either. I don't know if the addition of our Ahusaka brothers would be an asset or an obstacle if we came across any intent on attacking us."

"But why the oxen?"

"Oh, right." Judson trailed off as he adjusted the reins in his hand, steering the horses back to the center of the trail. "It's said they are attacking for the horses and mules. And those with oxen seem to get left alone." He shrugged, uncertain of the truth of it.

Marie scooted closer to him and placed her hand on his thigh, laying her head on his shoulder. She sighed contently just to be with her man on such an epic adventure. Judson turned his head and placed a simple but tender kiss on the top of her head. Marie bumped and jostled with every rock they hit and every hole they rolled into. She giggled, unable to keep her head still, so she lifted it.

"I hope when we arrive wherever it is we're going, we can build a home where we can grow old together and raise a family in the safety and peace of our new life together," Marie said dreamily, gazing up at the beautiful blue sky that was so vast, it reached from one side of the horizon to the other, not a cloud to be seen.

"Mmm, as do I. It is what keeps me going day to day out here in the wild lands—well, that and seeing you and touching you every day, not having to hide my love for you any longer." They sat in companionable silence for a while after that, simply enjoying the time together and seeing parts of their country they had never dreamed of seeing before.

"Oh no! Look! What is that?" Marie leaned forward, pointing off in the distance. Smoke rose into the sky, too far off to see where it came from and too much smoke to have come from a simple fire.

"That's a large fire. I didn't think there were any towns on this route for a day or two yet. I'd better alert the others." Judson let out a high-pitched whistle between his thumb and finger. Then he flicked the reins and shouted a command to order the horse to pick up speed. He directed the horses out of the line of the other wagons to pass along the outside, and made his way to the lead wagon driven by Butch and a younger boy named Dillon, whom they had picked up at one of their stops.

"Butch! See that fire yonder? Think we should check it out?" Judson called from his wagon.

Butch and Dillon both peered over at the pillar of smoke growing steadily larger as they drew closer.

"What was there is probably gone now," Butch said. "But let's make sure no one needs our help."

Judson pulled the reins, slowing the horses down so they could move back into the caravan line where the trail was smoother. As they approached, they could see more of what burned.

"Oh, Judson, it's another traveling caravan like ours," Marie said sadly, looking at the wreckage of what was once probably fifteen or so wagons in a circle with tents scattered around inside it. Marie sucked in a gasp as she gripped her forearms. "Witches, Judson. There were witches here . . . bad ones, if my stomach is any indication."

Marie held her arms across her stomach at the dull residue of whatever black magic had been practiced there. Judson frowned, and his eyes went on sudden alert.

"Do you feel anyone else about?" he asked, his voice low for just her ears.

Marie knew he was referring to Dante and the other witch hunters.

"Do you think this is the camp that man was from?" she whispered to herself, not expecting an answer. But then her question was answered. A tingling erupted behind her neck at the base of her skull, the recognition of another of her kind.

"There's a hunter here," she whispered to Judson. "Turn around. Get the wagons to turn around, now!" she almost shouted, but it was too late.

They were almost upon the still burning circle. Smells of gunpowder, burning flesh, and fear permeated the air enough to make even one with the strongest constitution revolt. Marie kicked herself that she didn't notice the signs sooner. She could have prevented them from being seen. It was possible another hunter could be in the area, but somehow she just knew it was Dante and his group. But why did they wait around?

Judson had given the secret warning signal by way of whistle, and the wagons all took off, away from the campsite and back on their trail, moving faster than advisable, but it was worth the risk to get away fast. Marie's foot bounced nervously, and her hands gripped the edges of the bench seat she shared with Judson until her knuckles turned white. She kept looking back, ensuring herself no one was following them. Marie hadn't seen anyone, but she felt them watching. She knew they were there, but why did they hide? Were they simply sending a message—an abhorrent and heinous message—or were they in the wrong place at the wrong time? Knowing her brother, she was sure it was a message sent directly to her.

Right as Marie was spiraling into guilt that she hadn't stopped Dante already, Alo peeked his head through the wagon tarps separating their seats from the back. "Darkness is in this place. A trap was set to follow you. We must be on alert. Cetan flies above."

Then he slipped back into the back without another word.

"Well, that was ominous," Judson said with a slight nervous chuckle.

Cetanwakuwa would serve as their eyes behind them as they traveled, at least until he needed to come down for a break.

"He's right. I can feel it. This is my fault," Marie said as tears now streamed down her face.

"No, this is Dante's fault. He chose. He could have chosen to live differently just as you did, but he didn't. This is his fault alone, Marie Marcella Blackstone," Judson said with such passion, Marie couldn't help but feel the love in her heart for him swell. She reached for his neck and tugged him to her lips, kissing him with such intimacy, she would have blushed if the others could see her brazenness in public. But right then, she didn't care.

When she pulled away, his eyes were filled with a starry gaze, but he quickly recovered, regaining his focus on driving the wagon. He checked his surroundings and the leads on the horses. He chuckled, then looked over at his wife. "I am proud to be your husband and proud to take on your name, Marie. Don't ever forget it."

She leaned over and pecked his cheek, then allowed him to continue steering.

A hawk circled above and cried out with an eerie call. Cetan. Marie felt a cold chill sweep down her spine and turned one last time to look at the smoke, now lessening the farther they got away. She could still see the outlines of the wagons—or what remained. It was a scene that would forever be etched upon her memory. But the sight of her brothers Dante and Isaiah, stepping out from behind one of the wagons and staring directly at her with hatred, was something else entirely; the sight was something of a nightmare. She gasped and held her heart. The thumping staccato beats were out of control. Fear gripped her as she watched Dante, not for herself but for all those she had grown to love who traveled with her. The promise in Dante's eyes told her this was just the beginning. Not only was he following them, but he was now hunting them.

CHAPTER 11

MISSOURI ~ AUTUMN 1851

*A*rriving at Independence, Missouri, without further incident was a huge relief for Marie. Though she often felt eyes on her, she never saw or felt anyone from Dante's group. Coming into a town after traveling the open trails for so long was refreshing. Marie soaked up seeing people milling about or on their way with purpose. Women strolled by in proper dresses, some with bustles and some with high collars buttoned up to their chins—a far cry from the traveling clothes she had become accustomed to seeing. The men wore top hats and suit jackets covering clean shirts with suspenders attached to proper trousers. Their group had been traveling for so long, they looked a little worse for the wear. Marie couldn't wait to get settled like the folks in this town were and wear clean and proper clothes.

Building after building lined each side of the main dirt road they traveled in on. Businesses such as the mercantile, the bank, a dress shop, a feed store, and many others boasted new goods, welcoming patrons to come and shop. Signs pointed toward the end of the road, toward the forge where they could find gunpowder, ammunition, and the blacksmith. Another sign pointed wagon trains to a large field area, where other wagons were parked. Judson followed the wagon in front of him in that direction.

Days went by, and Marie and her group rested themselves and their livestock. To their happy surprise, the other band of Stronghold witches were already there when they arrived. It was a joyful reunion for families and friends to reconnect and trade stories of their adventures on the trail. Rachael was happiest to have her coven back together.

The men had gone into the town and purchased new goods such as flour, rice, lentils, and beans. They also traded some of the goods they had brought with them from Virginia. The tobacco, homemade wines, and seeds from their garden were favorites. After the horses and mules had time to rest and feed, Judson, Hank, and Butch found ranchers who were looking to trade their oxen. They were almost ready to go.

"It's been so nice to be here, Judson," Marie commented one day, bringing down the clothes from the line. They had been there not much more than a couple months. "But I feel a restlessness in my spirit, a pull to keep going, to find where we belong."

Judson came up behind her, wrapped her in his arms, and held her tight. She giggled and dropped the linens she was folding and leaned back into him. Judson nuzzled her neck. "You smell good, woman."

"I hope so. I got some new lemon soap from a shop in town."

"I like it." He kissed the sensitive crook between her shoulder and neck. His mouth moved slowly and deliciously over her skin. She tipped her head back, baring her neck for him to continue. "I can't wait to find our home, but I know I belong with you no matter where we are."

She turned in his embrace and placed her hands around his

neck. Gazing into his beautiful warm brown eyes, she smiled, then stood up on her toes and tenderly brushed her lips across his, teasing him. He groaned.

"We don't get enough time to be alone," Judson lamented.

"And it looks like we don't get that time now either," Marie complained, nodding out toward the road where another train of wagons was entering the town of Independence. She stole one more moment and kissed him fully on the lips, a promise for another time in the future.

"It's a good thing Independence has a vast field for wagons. We seem to be quickly filling it up."

"I sense witches! I had no idea we would find more of them on our journey, not to mention the one group we had already came across. I'll go gather the others," Marie said excitedly and took off to find them.

FOR THE NEXT SEVERAL DAYS, the group became acquainted with the newest band of travelers, which included a coven of witches called the Luna Coven. Marie was excited to get to know all the new faces and to find others with such similar goals. She and Rachael had gone around and introduced themselves to the others. They had met a witch named Anne-Marie Beaumont—and her baby Saundra—who seemed like someone they would both get along with, but possibly might be someone Rachael could really learn from as a witch. Several witch families made up the new caravan, including the Beaumonts, the Bishops, and the Augustines —Raffaele and Priscilla. They were accompanied by a couple of vampire families by the surnames of Petran and Roca, and a few other families Marie could only assume were humans without boldly asking them: the Mills, the Alversons, the Fairchilds, the McFeenys, and the Stuarts. Marie found it overwhelming at first to remember who belonged to whom, as her gifts didn't identify more than witches and witch hunters, but over time she started to figure it out.

"Rachael!" Marie called, spotting her friend heading into the town.

"Marie, there you are! I was hoping I'd find you," she replied. "Come with me into town. I need to procure a few ingredients for a couple spells Anne-Marie and a few of the other Luna Coven witches are going to show me."

"I'm so happy you have someone else to trade spells with." Marie looped her arm inside Rachael's and walked with her.

"Where have you been?"

"I was speaking with the elders of their caravan," Marie answered, but her tone was hesitant and distracted. Of course, Rachael didn't miss anything.

"What's wrong, Marie?" Rachael stopped, twirling Marie around to face her, and pushed her over to a bench under a shop canopy, where they sat.

Marie blanched, and her gaze focused on a horse tied to a post across the road.

"We've discussed joining with the other caravan, but they are hesitant about traveling with us—with me specifically." She sighed, disappointment escaping in the form of a tear she had refused to shed until now.

"*What?*" Rachael asked in outrage. "Are they serious? What reason did they give?"

"I'm a hunter. In their travels, they've heard the Blackstone name, met others who had heard of Dante's destruction," she grumbled. "Much of their band are witches, and I'm a hunter. They have to think of the safety of all their people. I understand that."

"What are we? Buffalo? Shouldn't our history speak for your character? We wouldn't be here if you couldn't be trusted." Rachael crossed her arms in front of her chest in a pout.

"Of course you're not a buffalo, Rach, but they don't know me, and I can understand that," Marie said sadly.

"Well, then we will just need to prove it to them. We have a little more time. I think we may search for a more secluded place to make camp for the winter."

Marie twisted her face in thought. Rachael gripped Marie's hand and squeezed.

"We'll figure this out together. We're a team, you and I. If they can't see the value you bring, then I say we go on without them. We've come this far, and we can find our own place to settle."

Marie turned and fiercely hugged her friend. "Thank you, Rach. We are a team, but I have a dream of the home I might get to have in a place just like the one they're searching for. I'll build my own if I have to, but I'd rather build it with everyone here I've come to know."

"We'll figure it out. Oh! I wanted to tell you. I met the Augustines just now and Mr. Augustine—Raffaele—has the most beautiful ring he wears on his hand. I didn't dare ask, but I can practically feel magic coming from it. It's an elaborate silver setting holding a gorgeous moonstone in the center. Moonstone has tremendous psychic properties!" Rachael practically bounced. She loved jewelry, especially magical pieces.

"I'll have to see it. Come on, let's go get your ingredients. Maybe I can be your spell assistant," Marie said with a small smile and a wink as she tugged Rachael up from the bench.

BACK AT THE CAMPSITE, the women prepared several pots and kettles over three different fire pits, while Ahote and Dillon, the young orphaned witch, built the fires to light underneath them. Marie was concerned the Luna Coven group might not take to the

Ahusaka brothers as her group had, but the only ones they seemed suspicious of were Marie and her family.

One of the elders of the other group was a man named Elsmed —a fae—whose appearance was very intimidating. He seemed to watch Marie, peering into the depths of her soul, and maybe he could. Maybe he could decipher if she would fail in her pursuit for a peaceful existence as a hunter. She couldn't live with herself if that was the case. She couldn't fail.

Marie couldn't help but notice a few figures off in the shadows in what seemed to be a heated debate. Bishop. That was their name. She couldn't remember their first names, but she thought they were brothers; or two of them were brothers and one was a father. Though they were a part of the Luna Coven, she couldn't help but feel something dark in them, or in at least one of them. All three whipped their heads in her direction, as if they had been talking about her. Marie couldn't fathom why they would be discussing her unless they were plotting her demise—or she could just be paranoid at this point.

Suddenly, the campsite was stuffy and confining, and Marie felt a panic rise in her chest. She needed to be by herself. She needed to get away from all that was the traveling caravan and people speculating about her when they didn't even know her. Marie clutched her chest and turned back around toward the town. Evening was falling, and she really should have let Judson or Rachael know where she was going, but she had to get out right then.

She ran, not knowing or caring where she was going. Heading behind the businesses, she ran full out until her chest heaved and her breath was cut short. Back home, she used to run like that when she was frustrated, or even just for fun. She hadn't been able to escape like that since home—the home she would never return to.

Her heart hurt a little at that thought. It had been her family home for as long as she had known, and even before then. But home was where you made it and where you let your heart grow. She would find her home and make it something new; she was determined to do so.

Once she caught her breath, she slowly walked a little bit farther toward a barn set apart from the town. The moon rising above it was striking, and Marie moved closer to see the view behind the barn. She hesitated just before reaching it. Was it a good idea to go behind a barn by herself as it was growing dark? No, probably not, but Marie touched the dagger Judson had given her, now strapped at her side, and it gave her a small sense of security. With that in her mind, she slid stealthily around the barn, listening the entire way. At one point, she almost giggled at how absurd she was being. Most likely, there was nothing around the corner but the back of the barn and maybe a wild animal, but she could handle that. However, she wasn't expecting to find what she did.

Behind the barn, between the back wall and a large boulder, stood three figures. Two she couldn't quite make out from her vantage, but one she could. Dillon. The young witch who had joined their caravan months back. Marie's chest hitched. She didn't want to leap to conclusions before she had any facts, but the situation did not present itself well for him.

Marie held her breath and flattened herself against the side of the barn as best she could. She couldn't detect who the others were with him, but that didn't mean they weren't up to trouble. She listened, using her hunter hearing, which was much stronger than her human hearing; she had learned the ability to use each separately to save her sanity from sensitive hearing.

"Where is Dante? Is he here?" she heard Dillon ask in a whisper.

"No, he's waiting at our hiding place. Didn't want to be sensed too soon," another voice, a female, responded to him.

"What's the plan? What should I do?" Again Dillon.

"Do nothing. Keep your nose down. Well into the night in two days' time will be when the witches are at their weakest, and Dante will make his move. The witches' powers will be strained and so will their wards, due to it being the furthest night from both the new moon and the full moon." The second voice, a male, was more commanding.

"Thanks to your information about the wagon train not leaving soon, he will be able to make his move before they can escape him again," the female voice said.

"I get away with a clean start, right? That was the promise." Dillon's voice suddenly took on a tone of doubt. Marie didn't blame him. She wouldn't trust them.

"Don't be there that night. Dante is there to wipe out the witches and take back his family, but anyone who gets in the way will be collateral damage. Do you understand?"

"Understood," Dillon said, his voice weakened.

Marie hoped his decision weighed heavily upon him. She hated that he betrayed them after they had accepted him, the orphan of the group. Her cousin Caroline had taken a liking to him, and that he could betray her like that made Marie even more livid. She waited a few more beats, then turned to leave and sneak back until she was able to run without being heard.

She had to get back to tell the Luna Coven as well as her own people. Whether they trusted her or not, she would warn them, and they would believe her. They had to.

CHAPTER 12

"It could be a trap," the oldest Bishop said in a tone laced with casual indifference, yet with an underlying disgust that Marie would waste their time.

Marie had called a meeting with Anne-Marie Beaumont and asked her to gather the others, and she brought her group's leaders, consisting of Rachael, Judson, her father, Butch, and Alo. From the other caravan, Lawrence Mills, who Marie discovered was a frost dragon shifter, stood with his arms crossed and a tight look on his face as he grumbled something about just trying to get attention.

"It *is* a trap . . . for us!" Marie reiterated to him.

The Bishop—Rodavan she thought his name was—leaned down to her face. "It could be a trap set *by* you."

Marie threw her hands on her hips, ready to battle anyone who not only called her a liar, but also insinuated that she would put her people, her *family* in danger. Judson stood behind her and placed his large hands on her shoulders, steadying her—making sure she didn't throw a punch or two.

"It could," Anne-Marie said, nodding slowly. She was regal— power exuded from her—and she was friendly, but not overly warm, yet there was something about her Marie trusted. "It could, but why would she endanger her own people with whom she has traveled for this long? What is her gain?"

The group was silent for a moment.

"I know I'm biased toward Marie," Judson interjected. "But I also know her brother. He will stop at nothing to accomplish his goal, no matter how insane or absurd it may sound. There is no reasoning and no rationality at this point. I'm afraid his humanity is hanging on by a thread, if at all," Judson said with sensitivity, having Dante's family right next to him.

Butch and Alo went on to explain what they had seen on their travels to Independence, with the black-magic-using witches they had passed and the wreckage and devastation done by Dante.

The conversation went around for many more minutes, and finally Marie was finished. "Look, I know you don't know me, and you don't have any reason to trust me. But trust that I want the home you are looking for just as much as you do, and I will take my people and go out searching for it without you, if that's what you want. If you can't handle my presence—even though *I'm* the one fighting the feelings I get from your power every minute of every day—I understand. You should know the Stronghold coven has gifted us with spells that help control and subdue our hunter drives, but I still make the choice every day to rise above it. Even if we go our separate ways, promise me you will leave this place right away. I couldn't handle having your deaths on my conscience too. There have been too many deaths already."

Marie sighed. Everyone remained silent, contemplating her future or simply listening, so she continued.

"I want Judson and me to have a life, a family, one in which we can live peacefully with all different supernaturals. I want a home where generations of Blackstone witch hunters come after me, and I can leave the legacy of what it can mean to be a hunter without the actual hunting. So that's me. And we will be leaving in the morning. I hope you all will join us. I have enjoyed getting to know you and would never forgive myself if anything happened to you."

Marie stepped back and gripped Judson's hand, turning them both to leave.

"Wait," Anne-Marie called to her. Though her face was serious, a slight twitch of her mouth gave Marie the feeling she was impressed. "The Luna Coven and those joining us will discuss everything you have told us and come to our decision in the morning. Thank you for coming forward. I trust your people have the ability to deal with the traitor in your midst?"

Marie's throat bobbed as she gulped, but she nodded nonetheless. They had ways of dealing with traitors; she had just hoped to never need them.

"It will be taken care of," Butch announced, but the sadness in his eyes told Marie he had grown fond of the kid and was feeling the sting of betrayal heavier than most.

Marie and those with her left the meeting and went to pack up what they could in the dark. The rest would wait until morning. However, Dillon couldn't wait. They didn't want him to tip off Dante before they had the chance to leave.

Butch, Judson, Michael, Cetan, and a few others from the Stronghold coven went to restrain Dillon. Marie didn't have the heart or the stomach to "deal" with him, so they agreed to tie him up and leave one of the tents. Rachael came up with a spell and had one of her witches place it upon him so he couldn't yell for help. He would sit there and wait for Dante to show up, leaving him a message of their own.

MARIE, Judson, and everyone available packed up their camp and gathered all their supplies as dawn quickly approached. All except the Stronghold Coven who had been in the other caravan. Rachael came to Judson and Marie with tears in her eyes.

"The coven has decided to overthrow me. Well, they gave me a choice. I could remain with them or not, but they decided to stay and settle in the nearby region. They are finished traveling."

"Oh, Rachael. I'm so sorry," Marie said, gathering her friend in her arms. "What will you do? I couldn't bear to be without you, but I would understand your choice."

"There is no choice. You are my only family left. I go with you. I've already discussed it with Anne-Marie, and she will allow the Stronghold members who choose to go with us to join their coven," Rachael explained.

Marie held her friend out so she could see her eyes.

"Then it is settled. You will become an honorary Blackstone." Rachael giggled, which Marie was aiming for. "Come, we have much to do still."

Anne-Marie Beaumont and a couple Marie had recently met named Mihail Petran and his wife Irina—who Marie learned were a type of vampire called moroi—approached them.

"We will be leaving with you this morning. It is earlier than we had planned for, but the threat to all parties involved is more than we want to risk. We may need to stop for extended stays, depending how fierce the winter is as we head toward the mountains," Anne-Marie informed them.

Irina Petran added in her thick Romanian accent, "Though others may have speculations regarding you, we are willing to give you and yours a chance. However, some in particular—" She paused and cleared her throat. "Some have asked this be on a trial basis. I'm sorry, but it was the best we could do."

"So I just have to prove myself to secure the future we're all dreaming of?" Marie asked. "I could be offended, but it could be worse. I'll take it. I've proven myself most of my life that I could be who I wanted to be—and not who it was dictated to me to be."

Anne-Marie and Irina breathed a sigh of relief.

"Did you expect me to throw a fit?" Marie asked with humor.

"Well, we've seen all types, dear. You never know." Irina chuckled.

"Then let's pack up and depart Independence, Missouri. We have a destiny to find," Marie announced with joy.

MARIE HAD DEVELOPED a love for being on the dusty trail as they headed west toward the Rocky Mountains. There was a familiar lulling to the hypnotic rhythm of the wagons—that combined with the hope of a new day dawning gave Marie a feeling of positivity she hadn't known for a while. Things were looking up for her and her family. They would get their new start, and they'd have new friends to accomplish that with. The weather had grown chillier as the fall progressed into winter in the year 1851, and the wagon leaders from both caravans decided to go a little south on the Santa Fe Trail in hopes of a slightly warmer climate, giving themselves more time before they went into the harsh Rocky Mountains. They couldn't get past the feeling drawing them, pulling them, in the direction of the mountains. There was something there—they just weren't sure what it was yet. This trip was about faith, instincts, and a little bit of magic.

Marie had discovered upon dropping in on one of the meetings discussing direction that the witches had a strange little device that looked like a compass, but was bigger and had clock parts that made a ticking sound. She watched in awe as one of the witches performed a spell similar to a scrying spell she had heard Rachael do, and the little device whirred and lit up, pointing in a direction only they could see. It was part of what guided them on their way, and she loved all of it.

This part of the trip was much slower-moving than before—the big oxen simply moved slower than the horses and mules, but a strong sturdiness was apparent in every step they took.

"Oh look at that, Judson," Marie said and pointed out the vast grasslands of the prairie before them.

"It's beautiful," he agreed.

~

DAYS WENT BY, and finally by late 1851, they found a rare place of shelter amidst the prairie made of a cluster of tall rock monuments made of chalk to circle the wagons and set up camp, just far enough off the Santa Fe Trail to be safe, but still close enough to get back on the trail when weather allowed. Marie was pleased to see the few Stronghold witches who remained mingling with those of the Luna Coven. Rachael seemed happy having other leaders around whom she could share ideas with. Since her mother's passing, she hadn't felt comfortable showing her weaknesses in front of her own coven, though Marie knew them to be an understanding group. After all, they had taken her into their midst and made her feel like family.

"Marie!" Rachael bounded over to where Marie sat on a clay-like boulder. She stretched out on top of a blanket, having experienced the red dust staining her clothing earlier. "What are you doing?"

"I was looking over my family journal again. I can't help but feel like there's more to it. I keep coming across passages mentioning the awakening of the two pieces and wielding the weapon. I thought at first it was referring to uniting my human part with my hunter part—but I don't think it's quite that simple."

Rachael frowned.

"That sounds crazy doesn't it? Maybe I'm just looking for something because I desperately want there to be more to it, more for me to hold on to."

Rachael sat next to her friend and lightly ran her fingers over the leather book cover. "It hums a bit. I can feel an energy pulsing just under the cover. I think you're right," she confirmed with an excited smile.

"Do you know a spell that can unlock it?" Marie sat up straight with renewed anticipation.

Rachael twisted her lips in concentration. She then shook her head. "No, I can't think of anything at the moment, but let me think on it."

"Why can't I feel it?"

"I think because it's infused partially with witch magic. It's not dark, so you wouldn't feel it, right?"

"No, I guess not," Marie conceded.

A scream rang out of nowhere. The thought that Dante and his group had found them shot fear straight through Marie. She and Rachael jumped up and took off toward the sound. People gathered, and some rushed in to get closer, but then the line stopped abruptly. No one moved past it.

"What's going on?" Marie asked Caroline. The girl looked up at her with eyes reminding Marie of her sister LeAnna, and it struck a pain in Marie's heart to know that she may never see LeAnna again.

"Rattlesnake," Caroline said shakily, her eyes wide with fear. "Got one of the cows, I think."

"Everyone clear out. We got a rattler. No one goes near it until it's dealt with," Butch announced in his rough, loud voice.

"I hate snakes," Rachael said with a shudder.

Not a minute later, Ahote brushed up against her arm as he walked by and straight through the crowd to stand directly in front of the snake. Marie noted the chills that erupted on her friend's arm, and she nudged her playfully with a wink.

"He's being your hero," Marie whispered excitedly.

"Shh, I don't know what you're talking about," Rachael replied, before her attention was drawn raptly toward the tall Ahusaka brother with straight black shoulder-length hair he had tied back in a strip of leather. Ahote, which he had explained meant "restless one," was showing his bravery as he faced off with the desert snake. "He's so brave. I hope he doesn't get bitten."

"I'm sure he knows what he's doing." Marie thought he might in more ways than just with the snake. Her friend was slowly being wooed, and she didn't even know it.

The next thing they knew, Ahote was doing some kind of hypnotizing movements with his hands and the snake was in his thrall, as was almost everyone else. Out of nowhere, the hawk—his brother, Cetan—swooped down without a sound and dove for the snake's neck, severing the head cleanly off. The crowd gasped, also unaware of the stealthy move. Just when they felt they could breathe again, a loud bang shot off, echoing off the surrounding monuments of clay and dirt.

"It's all right, everyone. The boys took care of the snake. It's all clear," Butch announced.

"What was the shot for?" someone asked.

"Had to put the cow down," Hank added, now standing with his musket over his shoulder, next to Butch. "There's no coming back from that venom."

After the excitement, the crowd dispersed back to their daily chores or whatever they had been doing to prepare for the coming night. Marie watched Rachael cautiously approach Ahote and begin talking. It made Marie smile, another new dawning to add to her future hope.

AFTER WINTERING in the shelter of the chalk-like rock monuments, the band of travelers returned to the Santa Fe trail in the spring of 1852. Through the remainder of that year, they made their way slowly toward Santa Fe. After passing through what had recently become the Republic of New Mexico from the Republic of

Texas—now the state of Texas—the land grew in height with the presence of high steppe-like plains, and to the north, snow-capped mountains loomed with the threat of the coming winter. The farther they traveled, the more the land dipped and rose. Large monuments of rock grew out of the ground, with intense reds lightening to oranges and then to lighter tans as they reached the sky. They decided to remain there until the paths through the mountains would be less treacherous. The party grew restless, but ultimately found ways to keep busy and find work through the winter, saving up for the new supplies they would need in the coming months. Santa Fe had become a real trade route for furs especially, and they were definitely going to need those up in the mountains. Only time would tell if the pull toward whatever it was in those mountains they sought would grow strong again, or if Santa Fe was to be their new home. After much discussion, most still felt a restlessness in their spirits to continue toward the mountains, but for now they would remain.

CHAPTER 13

*E*arly summer in the year 1853, Marie and others had been working for a local farmer, when one day, she heard Rachael run through the field, yelling her name. "Marie!"

Marie and Judson both dropped their tools and looked up to see what the urgency was.

"What is it?" Marie shouted and ran to her friend, concern all over her face.

"It's time! The Luna Coven says it's time to go!" She jumped up and down excitedly. It was the moment they had been waiting for —the signal it was time to head into the mountains.

"When do we leave? We have to finish our work here." Judson spread his arm wide, indicating the jobs they had all taken on.

"End of this week. We have time to end our employment and obtain the supplies we need," Rachael informed them.

"It's time. We're heading home," Marie said with a large smile on her face, and Judson couldn't help but lean over and kiss her.

THE SUMMER in Santa Fe had been lovely, with desert blooms, warm days, and cool nights. Marie would miss it, but she kept her eyes on the horizon as they drove the oxen and the wagons north with all their newly acquired supplies. The mountains were calling them home.

Alo had explained earlier how there were what he called "dead zones" in these valleys. When Marie didn't fully understand, he went on to share how some of the local tribes had joined up with witches and put spells on some areas, as traps of a sort, to nullify the magic of those passing through. Witches wouldn't be able to cast spells, and shifters wouldn't be able to shift, but Marie wasn't sure what would happen to her, since she didn't have active magic. He explained it was to give the tribe whose territory it was the advantage and time to prepare. He reiterated how dangerous dead zones could be as they were getting close to an area where he thought one was.

An eerie feeling of foreboding settled in Marie's stomach. Something wasn't right, or perhaps it was just the way a "dead zone" felt. She couldn't shake it, though.

"Judson, can you give the whistle signal for everyone to stop? I need to speak with each wagon before we go any farther."

He nodded and gave the loud and shrill signal that hurt her ears every time. Marie jumped down from her wagon and ran to the lead wagon.

"What is it?" Anne-Marie asked from the front of her wagon.

"I'm not exactly sure, but something is wrong here. I needed to warn you to be prepared. I feel tingly all over, so I don't know if it's other hunters or just the dead zone, but we might need to be prepared. Have your weapons and spells ready as soon as we pass through the area."

"All right, we'll be ready. Inform the other wagons," she directed, and Marie did so, grateful to be taken seriously.

Marie knew each wagon was equipped with rifles, swords,

knives, bows and arrows, and an assortment of other weapons, many laced with magic, and many creations of Judson's. Once she was satisfied all had been warned and would prepare, she climbed back in her wagon, and Judson gave the whistle again to indicate forward movement.

It took longer than Marie thought it would to travel through the dead zone. An eerie silence permeated the arid air, nobody spoke, and all that could be heard were the sounds of the wheels tumbling over rocks and the clopping of the oxen. Just as they felt the dead zone coming to an end with an almost audible buzzing, Cetan jumped out of the wagon. He ran ahead to breach the boundary, transformed into the hawk, and flew to the sky to serve as their overhead eyes. Only moments later did the hawk screech a warning. Everyone drew their weapons as they came out of a narrow, open-air tunnel made of large sand cliffs on either side. The path opened into a wide plains area, where a line of wagons attempted to block the path.

Marie gasped and scratched at her neck at the same time. "Dante."

Her brother leaned casually against a wagon while those on either side of him had weapons drawn. Their faces were hard, and their stances ready to fight. They simply waited. She couldn't help but be saddened at the sight of her two brothers, Dante and Isaiah, her sister LeAnna, and other family members, some not even hunters, ready to fight them. And for what?

"Marie!" Dante called out. "I've been waiting for you. But it seems you are not nearly as surprised to see us standing here. I must have taken your ability to adapt for granted. I won't again. Father, Rodney, Michael, and Caroline, it's so nice to see you again. I'm ready to take you home, where you belong. It's time for you to end your foolishness now, Marie, and join me in the family . . . business, as it were." He sneered, the only indication of the madness taking over him.

"I've made my choice, Dante. You need to leave and let us move on," Marie returned.

"But your choice is wrong, dear sister, and I am here to right your wrong."

Marie could feel the unease trickle through the wagon train. They had tried to spread themselves out as wide as they could so they had a better chance. Weapons were drawn on both sides. She feared it would not end well.

"Dante, what you're doing is wrong. These people have done nothing to you. Let them pass unharmed."

A spark flared in his eyes. She had called him "wrong."

"Their existence is their sin, and they need to be punished for it. Don't you understand this is our purpose? This is who we are meant to be—the Blackstone witch hunters! We are to hunt the witches!" He was yelling now, losing his grasp on the thin thread of his sanity he held onto.

Instead of battling him, she needed to find a way to get everyone past him. Or at the least, she needed to convince him to leave, but she could only think of one idea to do that.

"Young man, many of us are not witches, and by your reasoning, we are innocent. Let us go through unharmed, then you may take your turn with the witches," Mihail Petran announced to the shock of many. True, he was a vampire, but perhaps this was his way of getting some of the wagons to the other side.

"Nice try." Dante lifted a brow. "You travel with them, you die with them."

He pulled out a blade from his hip holster, apparently a silent signal, as many of the others extended their weapons as well.

"Are we almost through here?" the elder Bishop droned as if the whole situation was a bore to him.

Marie's mouth dropped, but the fire she saw in Dante's eyes at being disrespected by a witch must have been what Rodavan was after, because Marie could see the slight lift of his lip—he was itching for a fight, apparently.

"We are done when you are all dead," Dante countered, pointing his blade at Rodavan.

"No! Dante, this doesn't have to be this way. Let them go," Marie pleaded as she jumped down from the seat of her wagon.

"Marie, no!" Judson shouted, but didn't grab her in time. He jumped down on the opposite side and ran over to her.

"Let them go, and I will go home with you," Marie announced with a hitch in her voice.

"No," she heard Judson and several others add in shocked whispers.

Others now joined them on what would seem to be the front line of their side, coming down from their seats and out from the backs of the wagons. Marie could still see Cetan circling above, and out of the corner of her eye, Alo and Ahote moving stealthily up to higher ground, blending in with the landscape. She hoped they had a plan.

Marie calmly took steps forward, one at a time. With one last look to Judson, she gave him a smile—one that encapsulated all the love she had for him, the promise of their future, and that she would be all right. "This is my choice. I will find my way to you in the end."

Tears welled up in his eyes, but he knew it was her choice to save all of them. He would get her back one way or another, even if he had to run across the country. There was no home without Marie for him.

Dante watched carefully, waiting for her to spring an attack on him, but she didn't. Standing only feet in front of Dante, Marie stopped. "Do we have a deal?"

"Oh, Marie, we have no intention of making a deal," Dante said snidely. He grabbed her and spun her around to face the rest of them. He held her tightly against his chest with his knife at her neck.

A clap echoed around them.

"Dante, no," Marie struggled to say, a single tear falling from her eye.

"Shh, sister, you will be set right soon enough," he crooned madly. To those on his side, he said, "Do it."

Everyone simultaneously advanced, weapons ready to take out the witches. Except when they moved forward, they were blocked by an invisible barrier.

"You see, we are not naive and will not let you simply slaughter us. Be warned that we will fight back, and we will not have mercy," Anne-Marie declared, standing regal and powerful with her hands outstretched, ready to use whatever magic was necessary to defend herself and her people.

Everyone standing with her joined her at the line. Vampires held weapons, and shifters shifted. Even Lawrence Mills had transformed into a mighty creature—a sight never before seen in the desert.

He grew to about fifty feet tall and twice as wide, Marie gauged, eyeing the tip of his enormous tail. She had only heard of dragons in stories she was told as a child. But he was unlike anything she'd imagined. The top of his head was circled with a crown of thorns, and his already pale green eyes shone with a vivid brilliance. His skin had become grayish-white scales covering him head to tail. From his back extended a large expanse of wings. Lawrence was quite the contrast to the tans, reds, and oranges of the desert. Instead of smoke and fire emitting from his mouth, mist and frost spewed forth in a great demonstration.

Eyes from everyone on the opposite side widened in surprise and a little fear—apparently it was a sight they had not yet seen either. Several faltered in their stances.

"What madness is this?" Dante said with slight alarm. He took several steps back, pulling Marie with him toward what appeared to be a getaway wagon.

"They have the upper hand, Dante. Leave while you can," Marie pushed. "Your people . . . our family could be hurt."

Dante growled, obviously frustrated they had foiled his plans. "No, you will still come with me."

"Ready, witches?" Anne-Marie shouted.

"Let us be done with this already," another one of the Bishops —Dragan—interjected, his voice impassive and bored, but the light in his eyes the opposite, as they gleamed with a spark of dark desire and an intensity in focus.

Marie groaned in pain as her eyes found Dragan's. Why was his magic different? Could he be infusing it with dark magic? But just then, Dante grunted also and poked the skin at her neck, causing her to jerk back.

"Looks like one of your witches you associate with might have some secrets of his own. Naughty, naughty," he taunted.

"Shields down!" Raffaele Augustine yelled in a deep baritone.

Another clap echoed through the mountains, and Dante's people moved forward as if their suspension had lifted. The witches began firing off spells, and those with rifles kept them trained, ready to defend, but only if Dante's rogues broke through their lines. Ahote and Alo made high-pitched sounds as they came jumping down from their places on the hillside and began fighting with knives. Metal upon metal clanked. Spells were uttered into the wind.

Dante pulled Marie with him quickly to the wagon and pushed her around to the front. "Time to go, sister."

"I don't think so." Rachael's voice came from the side of the wagon. Somehow she had slipped through the lines of fighting and awaited them there.

"And you are going to stop me, witch?" Dante laughed in her face. She flinched but straightened her shoulders.

"Yes, I am."

"Get in, Marie. We're leaving." Dante ignored Rachael and pushed Marie up into the seat. She struggled to make it tough on him.

"You would just leave your people to fight and most likely die while you escape? You are a coward, Dante." Marie couldn't believe it took her so long to see his true fear.

Rachael began uttering words Marie could barely hear until they grew louder in cadence and the strength in her voice sounded confident, then she spoke them loud and proud. Her intent and her words carried strongly with power.

"I curse you, Dante Blackstone. Marie will disappear to you. You will lose connection with her and be unable to find her for all the days of your life. Your hunter will be hidden from you, and you will regain your humanity. I curse you, Dante Blackstone. Hear me, goddesses of sky, earth, water, and fire. Hear my cry and bid my words flight."

Rachael took out a ritualistic athame she kept under her cloak and sliced the blade across her palm, drawing her own blood, then flung the dagger end over end until it landed in Dante's stomach. It wasn't a fatal wound, but it would definitely slow him down.

Dante pulled the dagger out and flung it away from him. Doubling over, he fell to his knees as he tried to staunch the bleeding.

Marie took advantage of the distraction and jumped down from his wagon. She ran over to Rachael, grabbing her arm and running back toward their wagons. Several people Marie didn't know from Dante's side lay on the ground, hurt, bleeding, or worse. A few wounds could be seen on the witches' side, but overall, they were in total control and had the upper hand, especially when the dragon kept freezing those who came too close to the wagons and the young ones hidden within them.

Marie's other brother Isaiah saw her fleeing and was about to give chase, but noticed Dante on the ground and rushed to his aid.

"Retreat!" Isaiah shouted, and he loaded Dante into the back of the wagon just before he jumped in the driver's seat and took off. The other wagons in their group followed, leaving a trail of dust in their wake.

Marie ran to Judson and threw herself into his arms, where he caught her and spun her around just like he used to before they left Virginia. He held her so tightly, she couldn't breathe. "I thought I was going to lose you."

"You could never lose me. You are my home, and I would always come back to you," Marie whispered into his ear, before he took her mouth and kissed her with a fierce desperation.

"Is anyone hurt?" Marie shouted, once she could breathe again.

Cetan and Ahote approached. In Cetan's arms lay a limp Alo. Marie rushed to him.

"Hurry! Can anyone help him?" she pleaded with the witches, but no one moved.

Ahote placed his hand upon her arm. "He would not want that. He is at peace. We will let him go."

Though his words were strong and brave, his eyes held immense sadness. Tears streamed down Marie's face for their loss.

"May we take a moment to bury him in the hills he loved so much?" Cetan asked quietly.

Marie glanced at Anne-Marie, who gave her a slight nod. "Of course you can. Take your time. And we are so sorry."

"It was his choice to come and his choice to fight. He died protecting something he believed in," Ahote added. The two brothers took their fallen up the side of the nearest hill, where the sun would set upon him, and buried Alo. Once they were finished, the others joined them at their sides and took a moment of silence in respect, then headed back to the wagons.

"Load up!" Butch shouted, getting everyone back on track.

They had miles to make up for today yet. Judson refused to let Marie go as he tugged her toward their wagon, Rachael following behind them. Marie reached back for her hand and brought her close. She could feel Rachael shaking.

"What you did back there . . ." Marie started.

"It needed to be done. For the first time, my magic worked just as I intended it to. I could feel it well up from deep within. He should leave you alone now." Rachael smiled, but it was weak and uncertain.

"I believe your magic is strong enough to do just that . . . but, Rach, by cursing him, you tied the curse to you. So you're never allowed to die, or the curse will be broken and he'll come for us again."

"I know." Rachael gulped, the residue from her spell still lingering on her. She was spent and looked like she was about to faint when Ahote came up behind her and caught her just before she fell. Without words, he scooped her up and carried her to the wagon, where Marie knew he would care for her friend. Ahote caught Marie's eyes. She nodded her thanks.

"Marie," Anne-Marie called out. "What you did was foolish and reckless, but you put your life on the line for all of ours. You have our trust, and we welcome you and yours to stay with us."

She angled her head slightly, giving Marie a show of respect. When Marie looked up, she noticed all those with Anne-Marie standing with her, even the Bishops, who were skeptics from the beginning, each nodding their agreement—some more enthusiastically than others. She hoped one day to get to know them all more, but now they had a trail to blaze.

"Thank you all. Your support means more to me than you could know. Let's go home." Marie smiled when others cheered and agreed. They loaded up and hit the trail, a looming chain of mountains ahead of them.

EPILOGUE

*t took the caravan the rest of the year and into the beginning of 1854 to make it through the mountains. The journey was slow and arduous. Some of the humans had the roughest time with sicknesses that didn't affect the supernaturals in the same way. They even lost a couple who weren't affected by any of the healing spells and tonics. Blizzards hit them, causing them to camp in caves at the bases of the mountains for long periods of time, waiting for the snow to lift. Even though they used magic to assist in the traveling, sometimes Mother Nature won out.

The pull up the mountain grew stronger and stronger the closer they drew to the summit. No one knew exactly what it was that had been pulling them, but no one could deny the powerful force either. Evergreens and pines stood tall and thick before they thinned out again near the top. The path was often overrun with snow and ice. It grew dark early, and the sun took too long to rise in the mornings. Marie thought they would never make it. Until one day, the sun rose warm and strong in the sky. Snow began to melt, and tiny green foliage peeked its crowns through the cold ground. Spring had finally arrived, and they had almost reached the top.

It was spring, March 1854, when the caravan reached a box canyon nestled between several mountain peaks. They all breathed a sigh of relief.

Home.

The canyon provided everything they had been searching for—seclusion, space for shifters to roam, land for their homes and crops, all the resources they needed, and the perfect conditions for protection wards. Overwhelmed, they slowly moved into the area, eyes wide with wonder, excitement, and shock. It was real. Their dream of a place to call home was real, and they had finally made it.

MARIE COULDN'T BELIEVE they had actually arrived. They had set up the wagons and tents right in the center of what would be their new home. The air was cool and fresh, and the mountains held something magical. With snow-capped mountain peaks in all four directions, privacy and seclusion was all theirs. Building the town of homes and businesses would take time, but she was excited about the prospects.

Upon arriving, they had been compelled to the northwest corner, where the magical pull was the strongest. A waterfall nearly three hundred feet high roared with the melting snow from the mountain it was cozy with. The falls poured into a pond surrounded by forest and large boulders; it was the most serene setting Marie had ever seen. A magical energy emanated from the falls itself and wafted into the town. Rachael had speculated that that energy was what pulled them from the very beginning.

With Marie and Judson's experience working the land and growing strong tobacco crops and vineyards back in Virginia, they had been granted land at the lower edge of one of the mountains, where the base met the plateau of the town, to grow a new vineyard and other large crops. It took time and magic, but Judson and

Marie built their first home. Judson had also built a lower room within the home that was hidden away, for him to work on his weapons. Her father Hank and her cousins Michael and Caroline were going to live with them until they had places of their own, and they would work for the vineyard. The house was going to be quite spacious, with each addition they had planned to make space for everyone. It was going to be the most beautiful vineyard Marie had ever seen as it climbed up the mountain. She dreamed of one day building small buildings where others could come and stay with them to enjoy the views—family, friends, or visitors, it didn't matter —she wanted to share her dream. It would be a place of peace where others could find tranquility, but it would also serve to calm her inner hunter when it grew challenging. Judson had also built an outbuilding for an actual forge to continue with metalwork for the town, as well.

Part of their agreement when choosing to stay in the town was that everyone had a part to play. The Blackstones' part would be threefold: to inform the town council if they sensed black magic, as it would not be allowed, to inform the town if other hunters showed up in the area unannounced, and to provide weapons for the town's use. Judson and Marie had agreed.

One day, at the base of the waterfalls, Marie sat reading through her family's journal once more. Content to put it away for a time, whether she found out the secret of the book or not, she wanted one last viewing. Dante was out of the picture—she hoped for a long, long time—and she had her chance to start over and define who the Blackstone hunters would be from now on. Running her fingers gently over the metalwork on the front, she stuck her finger into the depression in the middle, where it appeared something should fit.

An idea struck her, and she pulled out the dagger Judson had restored for her that had also belonged to her family. Examining the metalwork on the dagger, she realized that instead of them being the same pattern, they were each an exact mirror copy of the other, except where the book had a depression, the knife had a round stone set in the middle. Anticipation bubbled up in Marie. Could the key have been with her all along? Was it that simple? She placed the dagger face down on top of the book's cover and gently pushed the interlocking metal together like a puzzle. The stone on the knife fit snugly into the depression on the book. Unfortunately, nothing happened. Frowning, Marie tried it a couple more times, but the same result remained. Nothing.

She had taken her shoes off earlier and dipped her toes into the cool refreshing water of the pond. Dipping her hand into the water, she stirred it around her fingers. It wasn't warm enough for a dip at the moment, but she hoped to swim in it someday soon. Turning her focus one last time to what would become just a family heirloom, she pulled the knife free and ran her finger over the colorless stone; it was such a curious stone—she had no idea what it was. This time, when her water-moistened finger moved over the stone, it flickered with color. Marie gasped and almost dropped the thing.

"Do you need water? Or this particular water?" Marie wondered aloud.

In a bold move, she cupped her hand and brought a trickle of water, dripping it right over the stone. It glowed a bright blueish-green and actually absorbed the water containing it. Not knowing what else to do, she pushed the face of the dagger back into the metal work on the book and watched the two click together like a locking mechanism. The book hadn't been locked, but it unlocked pages that had not been there before—secret pages. It had now become a more personal diary, with grave details about the hunters and their powers, how to use them, how to contain them, how to not pass them on to human offspring, and how to control them and use them for good.

"I knew there was more to you!" Marie practically shouted in her excitement.

"More to what?" Judson asked, climbing up the pathway to where she was, carrying a picnic basket.

"My book! I figured it out!" She showed him all she had discovered. "Now I just need to read it all."

"Well, I have no doubt you will do that and more. Is there a section for you to add your own experiences so far? You should continue to document things for future generations of hunters."

"Yes, you are right. I have much to document so far. I also was thinking about the inscription on the dagger: Choose Yourself. I could see where one—a hunter specifically and in our case, Dante —would think it to mean choosing yourself above all else. But I believe it to mean I can choose for myself who I am to be."

"I believe you are right," Judson said with a big smile. "And have you?"

"I have!" She returned his big smile. "Did you bring me lunch?"

"I did." He placed the basket on the ground next to her and sat down. "How is Rachael adjusting?"

"She has decided to continue her training with the Luna Coven. She didn't feel she was ready to take over her coven, and they have since assimilated into the Lunas here, dropping the Stronghold name. It seemed like the best decision on all parts. I think she's happy. Plus, she's been busy with Ahote, from what I can tell." Marie winked at him with a devilish smile. "I can think of someone I'd like to be busy with." Marie flung her arms around Judson's neck.

He took a minute to admire his woman. But when she winked saucily, he laughed, then added, "I'm glad she is doing well."

Marie barely let him finish his words before she planted her mouth on his, kissing him senseless and taking control. They broke apart moments later.

"Should we have lunch?" Marie asked, quickly recovering.

"I'd like more of that first, though, please," he said breathlessly, pulling back from her strike attack.

He grabbed her around the waist and lifted her closer to him. Judson tenderly traced her lips with his own, keeping it light, teasing. Marie moaned and parted her lips for him. He wasted no time taking advantage of her open mouth and deepened the kiss, filling it with passion for Marie and their new life together. When she broke for air, she leaned her forehead against his.

"I love you, Judson Carter Blackstone."

"I love you too, Marie." He put her down and stepped back, still holding one of her hands. "There is something I've wanted to do for a while now, and since we are settled a bit more, I feel it's the right time."

"Oh? What's that?" Marie asked coyly, thinking he wanted to take their loving a bit further there at the falls.

Judson got down on one knee and raised a ring from his pocket. "Marie, my love. I know we are already married in the eyes of God, but we have never married publicly in the eyes of man. Will you do me the honor of marrying me once again, so I can proudly proclaim you my wife in front of our new friends in our new life?"

Tears streaming down her face, Marie was taken aback at the thoughtful sincerity of the man she had already chosen to be with for the rest of her life.

"Yes, I will."

Here in this new life, armed with new information and new support, Marie took a deep breath as she looked deeply into Judson's eyes. This was what she had always wanted. This was a new era for the Blackstone family . . . the dawn of the witch hunters.

READ MORE ABOUT the history of the witch hunters, coming January 2019. Also, you can discover Marie's descendants—the modern-day Blackstones—in *Reawakened* (A Havenwood Falls High Novella), available now.

We hope you enjoyed this story in the Legends of Havenwood Falls series featuring a variety of supernatural creatures. The series is a collaborative effort by multiple authors.

Books in the historical Legends of Havenwood Falls series:

Lost in Time by Tish Thawer
Dawn of the Witch Hunters by Morgan Wylie
Redemption's End by Eric R. Asher
Trapped Within a Wish by Brynn Myers
Blood and Damnation by Belinda Boring (August 2018)
Fated Beginnings by E.J. Fechenda (September 2018)

More books releasing on a monthly basis

Also try the signature New Adult/Adult series, Havenwood Falls, and the YA series, Havenwood Falls High

Stay up to date at www.HavenwoodFalls.com

Subscribe to our reader group and receive free stories and more!

ABOUT THE AUTHOR

Morgan Wylie is an award-winning and *USA Today* bestselling author with several genres published, from YA fantasy to adult paranormal romance and other things in between. Morgan published her first novel, Silent Orchids, one year after moving across the country with her family on a journey of new discovery. After an amazing three years in Nashville, TN, and the release of two more books, Morgan and her family found their way back to the Northwest, where they now reside. Still working every day with great optimism, Morgan continues to embrace all things: "Mama," wife, teacher, and mediator to the many voices and muses constantly chattering in her head . . . where it gets pretty loud!

You can find her and news on her books at the following:

MorganWylie.net
   MorganWylieBooks on Facebook
   @MWylieBooks on Twitter

ACKNOWLEDGMENTS

First off, I'd like to thank my amazing husband and my eight-year-old daughter, whose patience and support allow me to keep doing what I love to be doing, which is writing.

Next, I'd like to thank Kristie Cook, who had the amazing dream of creating Havenwood Falls and inviting others like me to come and play in her world. And thank you for the use of your characters the Beaumonts, the Petrans, and others; they were invaluable to my story.

Also, thank you to Kristie and Liz Ferry for your editing insights and expertise! Also for your patience as I attempted to challenge my thoughts and words from today's speech back into the 1800s.

I'd also like to thank Randi Cooley Wilson for the use of the Bishop boys, E.J. Fechenda for the mention of Elsmed, Amy Hale for the use of Lawrence Mills, and all the other authors whose characters made a brief appearance as a part of the wagon train. And to all my Havenwood Falls family, thank you for your tremendous support and encouragement. I'm thrilled to be in this adventure with you!

And thank you, readers! Whether this is your first introduction to the Blackstone family or you are a Blackstone veteran, thank you. Your support and time is most appreciated! And stay tuned for more from the Blackstone family in the future!

Thank You!

~ A Legends of Havenwood Falls Novella ~

HAVENWOOD FALLS LEGENDS

REDEMPTION'S END

ERIC R. ASHER

AN EXCERPT

Redemption's End (A Legends of Havenwood Falls Novella) by Eric R. Asher

Gregory and Charlotte left their lives as pirates behind to huddle in a tinker's shop, building fantastic creations powered by steam and aether. Fifteen hundred miles inland from the ocean they once called home, they only seek a quieter, safer way of life in the mountains of the Colorado territory. Fixing their neighbors' watches, creating beautiful and unique gifts, and helping to protect the burgeoning town is how they hope to make up for their past life of misdeeds.

Becoming a target of a crazed fae was not part of the plan.

The couple put their abilities and creations to the test to do everything they can to defend their new settlement. But their search for redemption from their wayward past may come to an end if death finds them—and their newfound family—first.

REDEMPTION'S END

AN EXCERPT

"How can you stand the noise in here?" Charlotte asked.

I kept my eyes on the seemingly random array of tiny gears and screws under the magnifying glass in front of me. Trying not to give myself away, I screwed the top back onto the flask in my left hand and slid it under the workbench.

"What noise?" I asked. I pulled another lens over my larger magnifier and carefully screwed one of the cogs back together. Only then did I turn away and look up at my wife, not missing the subtle frown and crease of her brow above her light brown eyes.

"No need to hide your flask," Charlotte said. "Even if I hadn't seen your clumsy ass trying to hide it, it smells like a still in here. I'm sure that's just what our customers want to see—you drunk, Gregory."

I sheepishly held out the bronze flask to Charlotte. "Just testing."

Somehow Charlotte managed to take a long swig out of the flask without breaking eye contact. The woman knew me too well, and I loved it.

"Who are you making that automata for?" Charlotte asked,

indicating the detached body, limbs, and tiny gears strewn about the workbench. When it was assembled, it would be an intricately animated dancer. Now it was, admittedly, a bit of a mess.

I took the flask back as she handed it to me, narrowing my eyes and taking a small sip. The slightly sweet moonshine burned its way down my throat before settling as a fire in my gut. "This one's just for the shop."

"Another bauble without a buyer," Charlotte muttered. "You need to finish those watches. At least until we find out there's a fence in town for some of our . . . less legitimate keepsakes, as I don't think the bank will accept stolen art. We can afford two more loan payments on the shop with what we have in cash. Maybe. We've barely been here a year, and the town has been here longer than that. I don't want to leave a bad impression on the banks."

I pinched the bridge of my nose and took a deep breath. "I know."

"Sure," Charlotte said. "What you really mean to say is that you find working on those pocket watches boring. And I understand that, I really do. But you aren't getting paid by the city again until you finish the conservatory. And that's if those contraptions will even work."

"They'll work," I said. "They have to. With all the creatures . . ."

"Species," Charlotte said, correcting me.

I nodded. "With all the species coming here, the town needs protection. Werewolves and vampires are peoples' neighbors in this place, but I don't think they fully understand the threat a fae can represent. Especially the Unseelie fae."

Charlotte settled into the workbench beside me. It used to be we could share the workbench, like one giant communal space. But if I was being honest with myself, I'd grown sloppy in my old age. There was a method to the chaos, and I always knew which screws went with which part and what springs I'd removed from which frame, but to the casual observer, it was pure chaos.

But beside me, Charlotte's workstation was pure order. She could chisel and carve wood, building the most intricate locks and puzzle boxes you can imagine, from the picture in her mind. There were a few things I could build from memory. I preferred to draw things out ahead of time. So in addition to three dozen jars of screws and fifty different trays of tiny parts, my workspace was littered with paper.

"You sell many more of those puzzle boxes," I said, "I won't need to worry about fixing those watches, or selling moonshine."

The front door—a thick heavy thing with a great deal of intricate carvings—swung open. Some of the patterns were subtle, but if someone had grown up around the tinkers' guilds, they were sure to recognize a few. And if they had grown up in the company of pirates, they were likely to recognize the vague outline of the crossbones formed from old iron.

Theodore, my apprentice, glanced back at the hinges as he crossed the threshold. He'd let his sandy brown hair grow to the point that he looked more like some of the soldiers I'd known in the east than the neatly groomed young man I was used to.

"You finally got the hinges to stop squeaking? They didn't even whisper."

The door snapped closed a moment later, and welcome chimes sounded. While I may have been able to fix the squeaking hinges, I was still having trouble regulating the volume of the chimes. They thundered to life, playing a quick four-note arpeggio that one might mistake for a thunderclap.

Theodore threw his hands over his ears, but by the time he managed to cover them, the chime was already done.

"Sorry about that," I said.

"What?" Theodore asked, slowly lowering his hands.

"I changed my mind," Charlotte said. "I think you should focus on fixing that damn chime."

"All in good time," I said, shooting her a crooked smile.

I stood up from the bench, carefully lifting the leather apron over my head. It held nearly as many tools as I had strewn across the workbench. "Ready for a little hike?"

"I'm ready to learn how to run those stills," Theodore said.

Charlotte slowly raised an eyebrow. "I believe what Theodore means is that he'd like to learn how to run the stills without blowing himself up."

I frowned slightly and nodded. "As I said."

I hung the apron on a small rack sunk into the wall. I pulled a discreet lever, capped with a polished walnut handle, and the entire rack sank into the wall, only to be replaced by a display of some of Charlotte's finest puzzle boxes.

"How cold is it today?" Charlotte asked.

"You haven't been out?" Theodore asked.

Charlotte shook her head. "Haven't needed to yet. Living above the shop is rather convenient like that."

"I'd say it's close to sixty."

"Take your coat," Charlotte said, eyeing me as I circled around the workbench very much without my coat.

"I don't think that's really necessary," I said.

"It doesn't matter if you think it's necessary," Charlotte said. "Take your coat."

I blinked at my wife, and while I pondered arguing for a moment, I instead hurried to the back, grabbed my coat, and joined Theodore in the front of the store. "We'll be back in a few hours."

"If you're not," Charlotte said, "I'll assume you're dead."

Theodore laughed, but he shut up when I shot him a cutting glare.

I rolled the cuff of my coat back and checked the watch sewn into the lining. It would likely take a half hour to hike to the stills if we didn't run into trouble. That would give us two hours before we needed to head back. "I'll take you out for a fine dinner tonight," I said.

Charlotte harrumphed. "As long as you're not cooking it, it should be fine indeed."

I leveled my gaze at her. "Charlotte."

She grinned at me and shooed us out the front door. I sighed when the chimes sounded again as the door closed behind us.

"Let's get on with it then," I said.

Most of the town had gravel streets now, but a few places tended to get muddy enough to trap a wagon wheel. I glanced back at the shop as my boots crunched in the rock. When we first opened the store, it had been my decision to simply put up a sign that said horologist. Charlotte protested, saying too many people wouldn't realize that we even sold watches, much less puzzle boxes and automata. As usual, she'd been right. So below the word horologist, we now had gilt lettering that said, "Timepieces, Music Boxes & Gifts."

I took a deep breath and smiled at the brick façade lined with rich lumber. It had long been our dream to leave our old seafaring life behind and open a shop, and it gave me hope that life would be good in this new town.

"You okay?" Theodore asked, pulling me out of my thoughts.

"I'm excellent, son," I said, pulling my coat a little tighter against a chilly breeze. "Into the woods."

Purchase *Redemption's End* by Eric R. Asher at your favorite book retailer.

www.ingramcontent.com/pod-product-compliance
Lightning Source LLC
Chambersburg PA
CBHW052006170626
46808CB00007B/2802